MW00577715

Hazard
in
Hawaii

A Doctor Danger Mystery

Welcome to the mysteries!

Heather Silvio

HEATHER SILVIO

Panther Books

Panther Books: Tampa, FL & Portland, OR.

Visit the author's website at https://www.heathersilvio.com
Contact the author at: heather@heathersilvio.com

Cover design by Sonia Freitas at Chloe Belle Arts
https://www.ChloeBelleArts.com

Library of Congress Control Number: 2021910203
ISBN (Print) 9781951192143
ISBN (E-book) 9781951192136

BOOKS BY HEATHER SILVIO

PARANORMAL TALENT AGENCY

Lights, Camera, Action (Episode One)

Reset to One (Episode Two)

That's a Wrap (Episode Three)

An Unexpected Sequel (Episode Four)

Jumping the Shark (Episode Five)

The Season Finale (Episode Six)

Paranormal Talent Agency Episodes 1-3 Collection

Paranormal Talent Agency Episodes 4-6 Collection

Paranormal Talent Agency Episodes 4-6 Collection

NON-SERIES FICTION

Not Quite Famous: A Romantic Comedy of an Actress
on the Edge

Beyond the Abyss: Tales of the Supernatural

Courting Death

NONFICTION

Special Snowflake Syndrome: The Unrecognized
Personality Disorder Destroying the World

Happiness by the Numbers: 9 Steps to Authentic
Happiness

Stress Disorders: A Healing Path for PTSD

CHAPTER ONE

Traveling to Hawaii to solve an unexplained overheating death had to be the most creative excuse for delaying the completion of my dissertation. This case would be a wild ride, I imagined. And then I'd finish my dissertation on the paranormal in mythology.

One day soon I'd be Sarah Danger, PhD. But, right now, I was Sarah Danger, Private Investigator Assistant. A giggle threatened to erupt at the craziness of being flown to Hawaii by a client. Freaking Hawaii.

"Would you like a complimentary Mai Tai?" The flight attendant balanced her tray of red-orange tropical cocktails and gave us a big smile. Her bright red lips were the only makeup on a youthful face surrounded by curly black hair. I ran a hand through my long wavy auburn hair, wondering how it would be if it curled like that.

"Definitely," I enthused and carefully received the fruity-smelling concoction from her. We'd been flying for over ten hours, traveling from Tampa to Hilo, via Los Angeles and Honolulu, and a refreshing alcoholic beverage sounded heavenly. My seatmate didn't respond, surprising me. "Jeff?"

"Sure," he finally replied, giving the flight attendant a tired smile. His hand shook for a moment before steadying, and he took the offered cocktail. "Don't give me that look," he admonished me as the flight attendant continued down the aisle. "It's just jet lag."

I narrowed my green eyes and considered my boss. Jeffrey McCarthy, 54 years old, with disheveled graying brown hair and a bit of stubble on pale skin that made him appear unwell. I supposed it might be jet lag. Although the teal-trimmed seats were comfortable, as a larger ex-athlete, he looked a little squished.

I, on the other hand, fit fine. There had to be some benefit to being child-size. After all, I stopped growing at the age of thirteen. But, the hours of travel across multiple time zones could exhaust anyone.

"Why don't you review our case before we land," he said into my silence. "Then we can lay out our plan of attack."

"Got it, boss." I opened my laptop and clicked on the JM Investigations folder. One more click on a folder labeled Andrea Helms, and the case opened before me. Such that it was. Andrea knew Jeff from church and knew he was a private investigator. Yesterday – could it have been only yesterday? – Andrea called Jeff in a panic about her little brother, Cameron, living in Hawaii.

Cameron had told her he'd read a story about a man in his town who died from overheating. The man's hyperthermia had no external cause and responded only minimally to medical attempts to cool him. Cameron was worried because he noticed he'd started having serious symptoms, too. He'd reported feeling warm, without exertion, and with the air conditioning running normally. That soon became sweating, clammy skin, and nausea. He thought it was a flu bug until he saw the article and something clicked. Andrea swore her brother wasn't a hypochondriac, and the doctor in the article had been baffled by what had happened. So, when she heard the worry in his voice, she told him to go to the hospital, where he was now being treated by the same doctor who saw the man who'd died. And then she called Jeff.

That's what we had: Andrea's concern, her brother's symptoms, and a single newspaper article about a mysterious hyperthermia death. "Not that I'm looking a gift trip to Hawaii in the mouth, so to speak, but is this a case for us?"

Jeff slow-blinked before responding. "Honestly? Not sure. That's why we're going to check it out. Determine if it's an unusual case." That was code for unexplained, likely supernatural, cases. And he was right. Which of course was why he'd accepted the case.

"Do you think she wants someone there to keep an eye on her brother?" Normally, regardless of a possible

3

supernatural element, we'd make a bunch of phone calls before flying halfway around the world. Except Andrea had told Jeff that she would not risk losing Cameron, her only remaining family. She'd rather spend the money and look foolish than risk his life. Jeff, being a sucker for a sob story, took the case even though it seemed medical and there would be nothing for us to find.

"Possibly," he conceded.

"Though it is bizarre." I opened the electronic file of the newspaper article that had triggered the frantic phone calls. Alan Richards had gone to the Emergency Department reporting an unresponsive-to-over-the-counter-medication fever. When the nurse first took his temperature, it registered as 104. They tried cooling blankets, IV fluids, and antibiotics, assuming they'd reduce the fever, assuage his concern, and send him home. Instead, his temperature continued to rise, topping out at 110 before his insides boiled and he died. I gulped some of my tropical cocktail, trying to tamp down a phantom bit of heating, enjoying the feel of the cool liquid down my throat.

The article reported that the medical examiner's office would perform an autopsy and take tissue and blood samples to determine the underlying cause of death. Possibly by the time we landed, they'd already know the cause, and the mystery would be solved. I wondered if we'd get to turn this into a little vacation, if so. Hey, it took me 32 years to make it to Hawaii; I wanted to enjoy it.

"What should we do first?" Jeff asked.

I smirked at his obvious attempt to get me to take lead. He often told me how great my analytical mind was – though much of it had to do with my ability. Since I was a kid, I could sense the emotions of others. I thought I was just highly empathic, and that lots of people were like that. Over the years, and in particular once I went through puberty, it became clear it was so much more.

According to my mother, and confirmed by internet research, I possessed clairempathy. It's in the realm of clairvoyance and is another form of extrasensory perception. It wasn't solely an empath's understanding of another. Others' emotional and physical experiences overwhelmed me, and I only distinguished them from my own with serious effort. The ability fully developed once I reached adulthood; it could be pretty freaky, to be honest. My mother taught me to keep an internal wall of protection built at all times to limit people's experiences day-to-day. With powerful reactions, though, that wall developed gaps or even crashed down.

Anyway, Jeff planned to retire so he could spend more time on a not-yet-purchased boat, and wanted to gift me the business. But I wasn't a licensed private investigator, nor was I interested in being licensed. This was a fun side job to pay for expenses while I earned my degree. It had helped pay for my Master's in Counseling, as well, so Jeff and I had known each other for over six years.

"The obvious place to start," I humored him, "would be with interviewing Dr. Michael Wilhelm, the doctor who saw Alan Richards and is now treating our client's brother.

Then our client's brother, Cameron Helms, and finally, the surviving spouse, Helen Richards." I ticked the three off on my fingers as I listed them. "Then we see where we are."

A flight attendant's voice sounded over the loudspeaker, asking everyone to be sure they'd stowed their carry-on articles and to prepare for landing.

"Perfect timing," Jeff said, with a wan smile. "And perfect plan of action."

I returned his smile before shifting my gaze past his face to look out the window. The turquoise water mesmerized; a beautiful sheet broken up with tiny white dots that became clearer as cresting waves. Soon that became a vibrant green, the land undulating with what appeared to be hills and valleys. When I thought of Hawaii, I pictured white sand beaches and smelled the scent of coconut. But we were landing on The Big Island of Hawai'i, home to the active volcanoes of Hawai'i Volcanoes National Park and Moana Key, the highest mountain peak in the United States. I'd been fascinated to learn that the Big Island of Hawai'i was spelled the traditional Hawaiian way, while the state itself remained the federally-recognized Hawaii.

At the sight of the high mountain peaks, all linguistic ruminations fled, and I wondered how close I could get to the lava of an active volcano. An involuntary shiver rolled over me at the thought of the heat and power.

CHAPTER TWO

Jeff and I made our way through Hilo International Airport, carry-on bags in tow, backpacks with laptops seeming to weigh double what they did when we started. It was amazing how just sitting tired you out. The weather in early December felt much like Florida when we stepped outside, mid-seventies with humidity. We read signs as we walked, following them to a low-slung building that housed the rental car companies. Soon, we had our stuff stowed in a nondescript SUV and we headed toward the freeway.

When most people think of Hawaii, they don't think of how big the island of Hawai'i truly is. Hilo is both hours away from the Kona coast (home of Kona coffee and sandy beaches) and forty minutes or so from Hawai'i Volcanoes National Park in the opposite direction. Our destination was Mountain Eden, a mid-size city more or less equidistant from the airport and the park. Our client's brother, Cameron Helms, and the recently deceased, Alan Richards, both resided there.

Big enough to house a major medical center, but still small enough to keep a small-town feel, or at least the internet said so. We eased off HI-11 and watched for a grocery store. One benefit of renting an actual house or condo was the kitchen. No need to eat out constantly. In contrast to my preconceived notions, the amount of greenery astounded. At the slower speeds through Mountain Eden, our headlights revealed incredible foliage not visible in the dusk while we drove at 60 MPH on the intrastate. We popped in and out of the grocery store, marveling at the increased cost of the food. There was a reason that commercials had fine print at the bottom stating prices may be higher in Hawaii and Alaska. A few more turns after exiting the parking lot and we pulled into the gravel driveway of the vacation rental we snagged for this trip.

A one-story wood-sided house greeted us. I expected from the pictures on the website where we booked the home that it was a lovely olive green that blended with the surrounding forest beautifully. Reality didn't disappoint. A moss-covered walkway led to the front door. A small, lettered sign read Peridot Palace, and I smiled at the play on words. I remembered from my brief research that peridot was the state gemstone, a delightful shade of green. And while a decent size, this house was no palace. Two sets of two keys on rings sat in an uncovered clay pot. Jeff handed me one set and then unlocked the forest green door. We stepped into a quaint wood-paneled foyer. To the left and right were closed doors to the two suites contained within the house.

"Take fifteen to unwind and unpack, then head to dinner and maybe meet some locals?" Jeff asked.

I agreed and we unlocked our respective doors. The suite had four rooms – galley kitchen, sitting area, bedroom, and bathroom. Terracotta flooring ran throughout, giving the small wood-paneled space some warmth, which was good, because the air had a bit of a chill. The temperature fell at night; I guessed this meant that the house was well-insulated enough to hold on to the coolness over the course of the day. I rolled my suitcase into the bedroom, happy to see two sets of windows. Hopefully, that meant tons of natural light awaited me in the morning.

Unpacking took all of five minutes, so I used my remaining ten to lay back on the floral bedspread, testing the bed. Plenty of pillows and a firm mattress suggested I'd sleep well here. That brought a smile to my face, before I remembered why we were here. One man had died, and another might be terminal.

Since the temperature had indeed fallen with the sun, I put my turquoise knit hat on over my long auburn hair and joined Jeff in the foyer. I didn't miss the smirk he tried to hide. Everyone who knew me knew I was a complete wuss when it came to weather. Under 70 degrees was cold. Period.

A quick drive from the house we found a locally owned restaurant for dinner, Kīlauea Rim, a nod to the volcano park twenty minutes away. Bigger than the standalone building appeared from the parking lot, the high ceilings with dark wood beams opened the space up even more. Which was good, because it was packed. Tile flooring that looked like wood ran underneath a handful each of occupied two-top and four-top light-wood tables, with a lone six-top anchoring the corner. Glossy photographs from the park added a nice touch.

We scored a two-top table along the far wall from the door – Jeff conceding that the cool air would come in every time someone came or went. I smiled at the consideration. My allergies meant candles were a no-go for me, so I appreciated the fake candle that provided ambiance with no smoke.

The waitress appeared from the back, brown hair in a messy but contained bun, a black apron over a white shirt and black pants, with sensible shoes. Her name tag said Marie. "Aloha. What can I get for you two?" Her pleasant voice held a slight accent I couldn't place. New England somewhere, maybe.

I ordered an entire small margarita pizza for myself and quirked an eyebrow when Jeff only got a salad. The waitress retreated with our orders and our menus.

"I'm not that hungry," he protested.

"You never eat salad." I took in his haggard appearance again. "Are you sure you're okay?"

"Would you believe I filled up on the plane?"

His joke succeeded in lightening the mood and I chuckled. "No, I wouldn't, but if you say you're fine."

"I do," he said with finality. He gave me a tired smile. "Let's discuss our plan of attack. I called to check on Cameron; it was a good thing Andrea had him give the hospital permission to talk about his medical status. There's been no change."

"He's unresponsive to cooling efforts?" Even though that's what the newspaper story had said about the original victim, I still found it surprising.

"Yep. They even tried an ice bath. Nada. Anyway, as I stated on the plane, I agree with your suggestions for our first three interview subjects. What do you think about splitting up for the interviews?"

"How come?" I couldn't remember the last time I conducted an interview on my own. Not that Jeff doubted my capability; he preferred to hear the words himself.

"In the interests of time, since we don't yet know the timeline of the first victim's illness and subsequent death."

I nodded. "We might be up against a tight clock."

"Exactly."

Not wanting to bring up his peaked appearance again, I decided to agree. Sort of. "We'll plan for that, and play it by ear. In case you're still having trouble with your jet lag."

Jeff gave a small sigh and a curt nod. That was likely the best I'd get from him. We finished our dinners and returned to the rental.

Light streaming through the windows woke me the next morning. I stretched in the bed, not wanting to leave the warmth of the comforter. Alas, my cellphone alarm kept blaring. Seven wasn't really that early, and I'd slept quite well in the new place. I scrambled some quick eggs and was raring to go when I exited the house.

My good mood evaporated when I saw Jeff, however. He looked worse than the night before, if that was possible. I opened my mouth, and he cut me off.

"Let's grab breakfast in a drive-thru on our way to the hospital."

"You didn't make breakfast?"

"I didn't feel like it," he answered, not meeting my questioning gaze.

I shook my head then followed him to the SUV.

Jeff's wheezing while we sat in the drive-thru lane was too much. "Jeffrey. You don't sound well."

He waved his hand dismissively. "I'm fine. I told you it's just jet lag. Plus, the humidity."

"We came from Florida."

The drive-thru worker saved Jeff from having to explain how the humidity in Hawaii's volcano area was somehow worse than the humidity in the Tampa Bay area. While he collected his food, I lowered my medieval stone wall of protection a smidge. I didn't normally use my clairempathy outside of professional situations, but Jeff was blowing off my concerns and he really looked ill.

Immediately I struggled with a heavy weight on my chest. I gulped in some air, ignoring the quick look Jeff shot me. He asked for and received some extra napkins from the woman in the window. Fatigue rooted me to my seat and I wanted to nap. My eyes fluttered closed and with effort, I pried them open. Then, I rushed to reconstruct my internal stone wall. Jeff was seriously unwell. There was no way I was separating from him for the interviews. I'd prepare to improvise if necessary.

Jeff ate his breakfast sandwich in silence for the final five minutes of the ride to the Mountain Eden Hospital Complex. The name was a misnomer, however, since the complex consisted of only two buildings: a main four-story hospital building and a two-story specialty clinic. We parked in front of the beige main building and followed the signs to the non-emergency entrance. This was good for me; without a sightline to the people behind closed doors, I couldn't pick up their emotional and physical issues.

Trepidation filled me as we walked to the Information desk to find out Cameron Helms' room. He wasn't responding to treatment. How long did we have until he died?

CHAPTER THREE

My worry about Cameron intensified when I saw him. I didn't need clairempathy to recognize he was ill. His greasy blond hair and beads of sweat on his flushed face told the story. He looked like he'd just finished an intense workout, not been confined to a hospital bed for the past 24 hours.

I remained closer to the door as Jeff approached the bed. We'd agreed I'd interview the doctor solo when he was available; thankfully, he wasn't free. That meant I could monitor Jeff instead.

"Cameron Helms?"

The man nodded in response to Jeff's question. "Jeffrey McCarthy? My sister told me you'd be in this morning."

"Yes, and this is my associate, Sarah. Are you up to answering a few questions?"

Cameron nodded again before frowning. "Are you okay? You look like I feel."

Despite my worry over Jeff's health, I still had to stifle a smile at Cameron's question.

"Just jet lag." Jeff dragged a chair over to the bed and collapsed into it. "Walk us through the past few days."

Cameron closed his eyes for a moment. "My best guess is that this started about three days ago."

"So, this is the start of the fourth day?" I asked from my lookout post in the doorway.

"Yes," Cameron confirmed. "Three days ago is when I first noticed difficulty with cooling down. I kept lowering the air conditioning over the course of the day. When my wife got home from her activities, she asked me why the house was freezing."

"How low was the A/C at that point?" Jeff asked.

Cameron's lips pursed in thought. "About 55."

Jeff wrote on his notepad. "That would be cold."

"Paula – that's my wife – put the A/C back up to something more reasonable, and then we took my temperature. It was 100, so elevated, but other than being hot, I had no other symptoms yet."

"What did you do?"

"I chalked it up to a low-grade fever from a minor infection, and took some over-the-counter medication."

"When did you realize it was more?"

"The next morning, I started feeling physically ill. Mild nausea, headache, pretty tired. I took more meds and rechecked my temperature. It was up another degree. Now,

Paula and I were more alarmed, but still assumed it must be some kind of infection. Then I saw the article about that guy who overheated and died." Cameron audibly swallowed and his face paled beneath the flush.

Jeff nodded. "We've read the article, though we haven't spoken with anyone about him."

"I could tell the story rattled Paula. Then, as you probably already know, I called my sister to get her opinion." He gave a weak smile, his bottom lip pulling in from a pronounced overbite. "She insisted I come to the hospital."

"And when Andrea is insistent," Jeff said, "you do what she says." The men shared a knowing smile.

"At the ER, they did a full lab check and tried administering a cooling IV. I think they also threw in an antibiotic. Everything came back normal – except the temperature. When I mentioned the death I'd read about, they knew all about it. He'd been treated here, which I didn't remember from the article. They admitted me since they couldn't identify the cause of the fever. Yesterday it was up another degree. And this morning, another." His voice dropped to a whisper on the last words and his fear pushed against my protection wall.

I performed the mental math and concluded he now had a 103-degree fever. Sustaining that could result in system damage, including brain damage. No wonder he looked awful.

Jeff noted that, then bit the tip of his pen. "Did anything unusual happen at the time you first felt hot?"

Cameron was shaking his head in the negative before Jeff even finished the question. "I've gone through it in my mind over and over. There's nothing. I work from home and didn't leave the house, so I wasn't around anybody new. Paula spent the day hiking in the park. When she came home, we watched television while we had dinner, and then went to bed. I have absolutely no idea what caused this."

Despite his matter-of-fact statements, I heard the fear in his voice. Now, something else poked at my protection wall. "Any new stresses? Anything related to work or family?"

"Work is great, nothing new there." He paused. "Family is me and my wife. Everything's normal there, too."

My head tilted. That wasn't right. A strong negative emotional undercurrent nudged my protection wall. "Where is Paula?"

Cameron's lips thinned for a moment, before he offered a small smile. "I insisted she go home and get some rest."

I wondered about the veracity of the statement, but moved on. "You said you first noticed the elevated temperature the day Paula hiked at the park. Volcanoes National Park?"

He nodded.

"Why didn't you go with her?"

Another pause. "She wanted to hike alone, for some self-care time. Plus, I had a project to finish for work."

Something seemed off. I removed a few stone blocks from my protection wall. Sadness competing with anger came off Cameron in waves and welled up in me. I tamped down the intense desire to yell and cry, to rail against… something. But he maintained his poker face. I decided not to press the issue and replaced my stone blocks.

After years of practice, almost like a meditation, taking the stones down from my protection wall was pretty easy. Replacing them could be trickier, especially when differentiating between what was me and what was another's strong physical and emotional reactions.

Though I would mention Cameron's internal fight to Jeff later.

"Do you know Alan Richards, the man who died?" Jeff asked.

"Not that I'm aware of."

"What about anything or anybody in common?"

"Not that I'm aware of," he repeated.

"Knock, knock," came a voice from behind me. I turned to see a middle-aged man in a white coat with curly black hair and dark eyes. "How're you doing, Cameron?"

"You tell me, Dr. Wilhelm."

The doctor hesitated.

"They can stay," Cameron added.

With a nod, the doctor explained that other than confirming the latest one-degree increase in temperature – by checking every hour – everything else seemed normal. No apparent damage. Yet.

The patient sighed. "Thanks. I guess."

"Hang in there while we figure this out." Dr. Wilhelm smiled, lighting up his entire face. He stepped toward the door to leave.

"Do you mind if we chat with you to confirm a few things?" Jeff asked, rising from his chair.

Expecting the question, Cameron confirmed his previous permission to discuss his medical status with us. "But can you do it outside the room?" He yawned. "I need a nap." His eyes were already closing as he finished the sentence.

I frowned before following the doctor and my boss into the hallway, glad that Jeff apparently forgot his preference that we divide and conquer the interviews. Despite what Dr. Wilhelm said about everything appearing normal, I couldn't shake the feeling that we needed to move faster.

CHAPTER FOUR

Doctor Michael Wilhelm towered over me when I stood next to him in the hallway. He had to be about 6'6", dwarfing my 5'2" frame. His thin physique, gentle demeanor, and beaming smile kept him from being intimidating though. I chanced lowering my protection wall for a quick moment, and basked in the happy feelings radiating from him. This was a man who loved his job.

"Thank you for speaking with us," my boss began.

"If the patient says it's okay, I have no problem with it," Dr. Wilhelm said, his eyes asking his unasked question.

"I'm Jeffrey McCarthy, a private investigator, and this is my assistant, Sarah. Cameron's family hired us to investigate his illness."

The doctor's brow furrowed in confusion. "Are you also doctors or scientists?"

"No; and believe me, I expressed that to the client," Jeff said with a shrug, then winced. Discomfort with the fact that we weren't scientists, or actual pain? "Since the medical explanations aren't coming, we're looking at other possibilities."

"Such as?"

"That's what we intend to find out," Jeff answered.

The doctor narrowed his eyes at the evasive response, but I could almost hear his internal shrug as he let it go. "What can I answer for you?"

"It's so cool, isn't it?" a loud voice interrupted our conversation. The three of us swiveled our heads to watch two women in civvies, with ID tags on lanyards around their necks, approach in the hallway.

"Right? Lava bubbling up with zero warning. How often does that happen?"

The women passed, continuing their animated discussion about unexpected bubbling lava. The thought of the immense power of a lava flow piqued my interest, and I planned to look it up when I had a moment.

"What can I help you with?" Dr. Wilhelm repeated.

"I understand everything has come back normal. Without divulging protected information, of course, how is it comparing with the first victim? I understand you treated him too." Jeff's voice dropped at the end with a wheeze. I opened my mouth to ask again how he was feeling. The slight shake of his head stopped me.

"When I saw Cameron, I recognized the similarities. What I can tell you is that no tests I've run have come back abnormal. To be thorough, like with my first patient, I sent samples to the CDC. Honestly, I'm not hopeful. I can't imagine they'll see something our lab didn't." He frowned. "If there was a true pathogen at work, there should be some abnormality that our tests would have caught. I'm certain of that."

"There were no differences between the test results?"

"None."

Jeff rubbed his left arm. A bead of sweat was forming on his brow, but it wasn't warm in the hallway. At all. I'd had enough. "Are you okay?" I asked, planting my hands on my hips, fully prepared to drop my protection wall again if necessary.

He waved his hand at me. "I'm fine. Jet lag."

The doctor peered closer at Jeff's face. "Are you sure? You don't look good."

"Thanks for that," Jeff joked, with another wheeze.

"I'll instruct the nurse to run some tests," Dr. Wilhelm said, his voice brooking no argument.

Of course, my boss argued. "I only need some water," he insisted. "Besides, I have a couple more questions."

"I'll answer your questions. If you'll agree to let the nurse evaluate you after," the doctor bargained.

"Fine, fine," Jeff acquiesced.

At his agreement, I relaxed my tense stance.

Jeff struggled to take a deep breath before continuing. "Do you know when patient zero first noted symptoms?"

"Patient zero?" Dr. Wilhelm chuckled. "That sounds like you expect this to be a contagion."

Neither Jeff nor I laughed. Who knew what this was or would be? We needed to identify the source of the … issue … as well as the connection between the two men. It must be there; we just weren't seeing it.

"Patient zero reported symptoms ten days before he died," Dr. Wilhelm answered Jeff's question.

"Cameron may die in seven days," I voiced what we all concluded. Today was the start of his fourth day.

"Much can change in a week," the doctor countered, "but, if nothing changes, yes, as a best guess, that is the expected timeline and outcome." His mouth turned down.

We stood in silence in the hallway, ignoring the hustle and bustle of staff, patients, and family members surrounding us. No medical explanation. No alternative ideas yet. If somebody didn't figure this out, Cameron would die. And possibly other people, too. I made a mental note to ask if there were others, and have Mandie, our researcher back home in Tampa, scour the internet.

Jeff opened his mouth to speak. He closed it after a short exhalation. His brown eyes rolled upward, showing the whites. Then he dropped to the gray vinyl floor like all of his bones had disintegrated.

CHAPTER FIVE

The next moments passed in a blur and soon I leaned against the waiting room's floor-to-ceiling window, staring out into the beautiful day beyond. The sun shone down from an azure blue sky, and the deep green plants and trees surrounding the building swayed in a light wind.

How I wished I could be outside enjoying that, instead of inside, wondering if my boss, my friend, was dying. I'd called Jeff's wife, Chrissie, once a nurse wheeled him away. She stood at the ready to fly out if necessary; I managed to convince her to wait until I got an update from the doctor.

A throat clearing behind me caught my attention and I turned to find Dr. Wilhelm. Cautious optimism radiated off of him, lifting the apprehension that had settled over my body.

"How is he?"

"Jeffrey had a minor heart attack—"

"Oh no!" My hands fluttered to my face.

"—but he never lost consciousness, so we believe he's past the acute danger zone right now."

"Thank goodness."

"We'll want to keep him at least two days in the ICU for observation. If he remains stable, he can be released then. If anything worsens, that could be longer."

I nodded in understanding, not trusting myself to speak. He would be okay. He had to be.

"Why don't you grab coffee or brunch in the cafeteria? He'll be able to have visitors in about an hour."

"Thank you, I will."

Dr. Wilhelm gave me the floor and ICU bed number for Jeff, then pointed me toward the first sign and arrow showing the way to the cafeteria. I decided to call Chrissie before going there. The waiting room held only one other occupant, and she sat on the other end, out of earshot.

"How's he doing?" Chrissie answered my call, every word saturated with worry.

"They're keeping him just for observation," I said, starting with the good news. "He had a minor heart attack. The doctor assures me he's past the danger zone." I rushed to add the doctor's exact words and heard her sigh of relief.

"You don't think I should fly out there?"

The uncertainty in her tone surprised me. She and Jeff had been married for 25 years, and she was always self-assured. I hesitated. "I don't. But I'll be able to visit with him in about an hour. I'll have a much better sense then."

25

She didn't need me to elaborate. She was well aware of my abilities. My clairempathy would tell me the truth about Jeff.

"Thank you, Sarah. I'm glad you're with him." Her choked-up voice hit me hard.

"Me too. He's going to be okay," I said, relying on the doctor's body language and emotional beliefs as accurate. After assuring her I'd call as soon as I saw him, I ambled my way down the hall, not in any hurry to force food into my twisting stomach. Although I felt better knowing Jeff was stable, I wouldn't be at ease until the hospital released him. Even then, didn't someone always have a heightened risk for another heart attack after their first? I probably picked that up off of a random website or a television show. A mirthless chuckle followed the thought. At least I knew not to express it to Chrissie. Of course, she was smart enough to have considered it herself.

A large sign over a curved archway and the aroma of frying oil announced my arrival at the cafeteria. The room held standard four-top tables in the center, with six-seater booths lining the walls to the left and opposite me. To the right was another rounded archway with three cashiers at registers beneath. I entered that area and took in my options. Refrigerators contained wrapped sandwiches, yogurt, small milk cartons like we used to get in school, and some plastic orange juice bottles. A counter lined the length of a wall ahead of me. Several workers stood behind the plexiglass, their hair in nets, doling out richly scented food to the few people standing before them with trays. I grabbed a tray and queued up, deciding I shouldn't pass up the opportunity to put real food in my stomach. What might the rest of the day entail?

After I paid for my omelet and hash browns, I took a seat in a booth, facing the opening to the cafeteria. It wouldn't hurt to be visible, even though I didn't expect the doctor to come find me here if anything changed with Jeff.

Indistinct murmurs from the handful of others in the room penetrated my awareness before I ignored them. My wall of protection thankfully withstood their emotional and physical feelings, and none penetrated. This allowed my mind to swirl with questions and concerns, beyond Jeff's safety, which was my priority. I wondered what he would want to do now. He wouldn't want to halt the investigation for two days, maybe longer, when we had maybe a seven-day window.

But the only alternative I saw was having me take lead. I gulped. There were so many reasons that was a bad idea. I ticked them off in my head. The big one: I wasn't a licensed private investigator. Would it even be legal for me to continue the investigation without Jeff? Because of the first reason, I'd never been lead on a case before, let alone one with possible dire consequences. And, finally, we still hadn't concluded the case had a non-medical component. Although I supposed the doctor had mostly eliminated that one.

After finishing my brunch, and with only mild indigestion from my frantic thoughts, I returned the tray to the conveyor belt that magically disappeared behind a wall for disposal. I followed more signs to an elevator to the third floor, then to the ICU. The nurse pointed me toward Jeff's bed, which was encircled by a pale blue privacy curtain.

Antiseptic smells assaulted my nose. Incessant beeping filled my ears. My protection wall strained mightily against the severe illness in this room. It was in danger of being breached by the intensity of the feelings in the room, and I had to work extra hard to tamp down the array of confused emotions making my limbs heavy. I directed my intention to the human behind the curtain, attempting to quiet all the senses from the other patients.

"I hear you breathing," came a hoarse voice.

That answered my unasked question of whether Jeff was awake. I smiled and slipped through a slight opening in the curtain, while leaving it drawn around us. The smile dimmed when I took in his appearance. His salt-n-pepper hair stuck out in all directions; wires crisscrossed his large body. His bright eyes belied his haggard expression.

"Don't look so worried. I'm going to be fine."

My smile returned at his assurances, mainly because of his infectious confidence. Plus, the brief removal of a few stones from my protection wall confirmed fatigue and worry, but no crushing chest pressure like before.

"You sure do go to extremes to get out of the tough cases, don't you?" I teased, pointing my finger at him.

"I've told you I intend for you to take over," he retorted with a wink. "What better way than to have a heart attack and a doctor order bed rest?"

My eyes rolled of their own volition. "I was afraid you'd say that."

"What am I going to say next?"

"That you want me to continue investigating."

"What argument will you make?"

"That I'm not a legal PI. That I've never taken lead before. That we still don't even know if there's a non-medical side to this case." I recounted what I'd considered in the cafeteria, and this time, I ticked the three reasons off on my fingers.

"And what will I respond with to convince you to continue investigating?"

I smirked because I knew what he was doing, getting me to convince myself I could do this. Despite having been described as an adrenaline junkie in the past, I didn't find leadership roles enticing. Just anxiety-provoking. Or maybe I was too much of a rule-breaker, instead of a rule-follower, to be a leader. I refocused on answering Jeff's question. "We're not official, anyway, since you're not licensed here."

"Go on."

I thought like Jeff for a moment. "I've got an analytical mind, so can see patterns and make logical decisions."

A small smile formed and he inclined his head.

"While the medical professionals work the illness angle, I'm capable of interviewing the people we've identified. I have a degree in counseling and I have my extreme empathy, my clairempathy." Until my mother explained its proper name, I'd labeled it extreme empathy.

It had been kind of a funny name, at least to me, and sometimes it still slipped out. The correct name required explanation on the rare occasions when I mentioned it.

"Anything else?"

I considered our operations. "We don't usually work alone; if the client will pay for it, fly Dan out?"

"I'm sure Helen will be fine with the additional cost; but, run it by her first."

"Will do."

"Are you ready to move forward now?" Jeff squinted, reading my expression and body language. He knew me too well.

"I'm scared," I admitted, crossing my arms in front of my chest.

"Of what?"

Silence descended while he waited for me to work through my fears. "Of failing, and people dying."

"What would I say to that?" Jeff asked.

My hyperactive mind considered his question. "That if I quit, the same outcome may result, and I won't have even tried."

"Exactly."

Confidence swelled within me. Although I couldn't tell if that came from me or from Jeff's supreme faith in me, I felt better. Prepared to face this weird unknown. I would do everything I could to determine if a non-medical, supernatural reason explained the unexplained fever-illness.

"I'm ready. I can do this."

CHAPTER SIX

After laying out my game plan for Jeff, I headed back to the cafeteria to make phone calls while he slept. I bypassed the food section and sat in the same outward-facing booth. The flow of people in and out seemed much the same as earlier. I did the math in my head on what time it was in Tampa and thought I was okay.

"Did you see him? How's he doing? Are you sure I don't need to fly out there?" Chrissie McCarthy asked her rapid-fire questions.

"Yes. He's doing well. And, I'm sure you don't need to fly out here," I answered in a calm and steady tone.

It worked. She sighed. "Thank you for keeping me sane. This is so hard."

"I know, but Jeff's in good spirits. It's just for observation," I reminded her.

"Are you in charge now?"

I heard the smile in her voice. "What do you think?"

"I think you tried to explain why you couldn't do it, and he made you convince yourself otherwise."

"You would not be wrong on either count."

She laughed. "You can do it. Jeff doesn't praise easily."

I flushed with pride, but also caught my breath at a spike in anxiety. "Thanks, Chrissie."

"Call me if anything changes."

"Will do." We disconnected and I selected the next name I wanted.

"Hey doc," Amanda Jenkins sang into the phone.

"Not yet," I reminded her.

"How's that dissertation coming?"

"I have more important news," I sidestepped.

"What happened?" Her tone changed at the solemnity of my own.

I brought her up to speed on Jeff's heart attack, emphasizing that the doctor considered it minor, he never lost consciousness, and they should release him in two days.

"You're taking lead."

"So, it would seem."

"What can I do on my end?"

Amanda, or Mandie to her friends, was our team's primary researcher. With three children under the age of thirteen and a library science degree, she was perfectly suited to a work-from-home job with irregular hours. We'd met in graduate school and I brought her on board with Jeff when his then-researcher quit for unknown reasons.

"You've seen the original article on Alan Richards, who died, and you have the information on Cameron Helms, currently hospitalized with a seemingly identical sickness," I summarized. "Based on their symptom profiles, can you scour the web for any other similar instances?"

"Anything that's made the news will be easy," she said, talking through the steps and challenges aloud. "And most posts on social media I'll find with my forager too." Oh yeah, Mandie had developed her own customized internet information scraper that she called her forager. "It'll get past some simpler firewalls as well."

I didn't bother to ask if that part was legal; plausible deniability, you know?

"Any notes in an online medical file will be protected enough for me not to be able to grab," she warned.

"I anticipated that, and am hoping the doctor here can call around to other hospitals on the island, if he hasn't already."

"Sounds good. Anything else?"

"Nope. Calling the client next about flying Dan out for backup."

"Uh-huh."

I rolled my eyes at her laughter. "Jeff agreed."

"I'm sure. That should be interesting."

"Call me with any results?"

"You got it, doc."

"Not yet," I responded before she disconnected.

The conversation with Andrea Helms, the client, started much the same. I brought her up to speed on the d Jeff, assuring her he would be fine. After giving her the ICU phone number so she could reach him, I got her okay to fly out Dan.

"What's up, doc," Daniel Trawl answered his phone.

"Not yet," I responded, a smile in my voice. Dan was a 22-year-old brand-new graduate student working toward his own degree in comparative mythology. After meeting him at the start of the semester, he offered to volunteer with Jeff's agency if he could shadow us and write up our cases for his blog. So far, we hadn't had a very interesting one for him. That seemed about to change.

"Do you want to come to Hawaii?"

"You're joking."

"Nope." For the third time, I brought someone up to speed on the case and Jeff's condition. Unlike the ladies, Dan had no concerns about Jeff.

"He's a tough guy who's never going to die," Dan concluded. "And, of course, I want to come to Hawaii. This case might end up being a good one for the blog."

Could I call it, or what?

"Or an academic journal?" He added the question as an afterthought.

"Possible. Check the flights. Try to grab the earliest you can to get out here that doesn't cost a ridiculous amount of money. Andrea agreed to Jeff's request, but we don't want to take advantage."

"Got it. I'll email you my flight info when I have it, doc."

"Sounds good. And, not yet."

34

His laughter came through the line before he ended the call. I rose from the cafeteria booth and headed back to the third floor, wondering how easy it would be to track Dr. Wilhelm down to ask him for my favor.

Much easier than I thought, since I spotted him the instant I exited the elevator. "Dr. Wilhelm," I called out and the doctor turned.

"Yes?" He walked my way and we stepped toward the wall, out of the general line of hallway traffic. Posture ramrod straight, he radiated competence.

"I was wondering if I could ask a favor."

"You can always ask," he said with a smile.

I asked about him calling around to the other area hospitals to determine if anybody else was sick with a similar illness. He was nodding by the time I finished.

"I've done that and am waiting to hear back. If there are any, and their doctors are as stumped as I am, I'll see if they're willing to check with their patients about sharing their names with you."

"That'd be great. Thank you very much."

"I don't want anybody else to die," he said, a shadow passing over his face.

"Me neither," I agreed, thinking of Alan Richards, the first victim, before handing the doctor my business card. He assured me he'd text if he got any news, then strode off to his next patient.

With a shock, I realized it was dinnertime. My calls had taken much longer than they seemed at the time. The chill when I returned to the rental home prompted me to turn up the gas heater before whipping up a delicious smelling Thai curry. After only a few bites, my phone rang. Mandie.

"Isn't it kind of late for you?"

"The kids are in bed," she answered, "so I was able to get started?"

"Fair enough." I swallowed a bite of curry. "What did you find?"

"Social media post about a woman who died; seems to have been posted by her sister, who noted strange symptoms."

"An unexplained death."

"Looks like it."

"What's her name?"

"Annalisa Webster. I'll text the name, address, and phone number to you when we hang up."

"Is she connected to either Alan Richards or Cameron Helms?"

"Not according to any of their social media accounts."

"Hmm, okay. Another unconnected victim." I drummed my fingers on the tabletop. "I don't believe it. Too big a coincidence for three people to have the same illness and not have anything in common. Grocery store, gym, favorite bar. Something."

"I agree," Mandie said, "but nothing's pinging. I'll keep looking."

"Thanks, I'll add her name to my list to investigate on this end. Maybe talk to the sister."

"Is Dan flying out?"

"Tomorrow morning, arriving late."

"Try not to have too much fun."

"Good night, Mandie."

"Good night, doc."

"Not yet."

I ate my curry, the television on in the background, while my mind turned the information we'd gathered over and around. What little, disconnected information we had, at any rate. A story on the evening news grabbed my attention and I hurried from the table to the living space.

"Volcanologists remain stumped by the continued unexplained increase in activity with Kīlauea in Volcanoes National Park. Although a known active volcano, less than two weeks ago, scientists registered a sudden rise in lava production and movement within the volcano." The newscaster's concerned facial expression matched her tone as she gave viewers the story.

That must have been what the two women at the hospital had been talking about. It wasn't too far from where we were staying. My assumption was that the volcano wouldn't suddenly have a massive eruption that killed us all. Probably nothing to worry about. I watched the rest of the news, cleaned up my dinner mess, and then got ready for bed. Sleep eluded me for hours. An unsettled feeling had crept over me, and I didn't know why.

CHAPTER SEVEN

Helen Richards lived in a sky-blue, two-story home with a fascinating combination patio-gazebo that sat between the levels, up a short flight of worn white wooden stairs. I stayed in the SUV for a moment, reviewing my questions. I figured I'd ease into it. After all, her husband just died and everybody dealt with grief in a personal way. I walked upstairs, mentally removing a single stone block from my protection wall to allow in a bit of her energy.

A thirty-something blond woman with a deep tan answered the door, her blue eyes taking me in with disinterest. "Yes?"

"Helen Richards?"

"You are?"

Normally I would be taken aback by her tone, but her flat emotional energy confused me. Maybe I didn't remove my stone block as I'd thought? I probed around the flatness; it made me want to shrug and head back to the car. I isolated the emptiness and wondered if she was dealing with her grief by squashing it. "Sarah Danger. I'm consulting on a case for a private investigator." I extended my hand in greeting.

Helen grazed my offered hand for a mere millisecond. "What are you investigating?"

"May I come in?" The weather had become cloudy and cold, with the air smelling of impending rain.

"No."

"Um." Her immediate refusal caught me off guard.

She stepped back and began closing the door in my face.

My arm shot out. "May we speak out here?"

A barely audible sigh. But she opened the door again, joined me on the porch, and closed the door behind her. Her tired eyes zeroed in on me. "What are you investigating?"

"Thank you so much for seeing me. And, may I say, I'm sorry for your loss."

A heartbeat delay before she responded. "Thank you." She stood with perfect posture, her arms dangling at her sides, the hands occasionally brushing against her jeans.

"Our client has a family member who might have the same illness that your husband passed from," I began.

Helen blanched at the sentence.

"A medical explanation has been slow in coming, so we're investigating alternatives."

"Such as?"

"We don't know," I hedged, knowing enough not to float the word *supernatural* to the grieving wife. "Do you mind if I ask you a few questions?"

She nodded her consent.

Flipping open my notepad, I decided to start with low emotion questions. We weren't meshing, and I wanted to build some rapport. "How do you spend your days?"

A door banged nearby, and both Helen and I glanced to the house next door. An older woman sat in a wicker chair on her porch, staring at us. That wasn't weird at all. Helen and I returned to our conversation, though I noticed she spoke softer when she replied.

"Breakfast with my husband. Work. Dinner with my husband. Some TV. Then bed. Or at least, I did." Her monotone voice belied a spark of anger that flung off her and made me want to slam my fist on the house. I isolated that emotion, as before, and reconsidered the wisdom of removing a stone block from my protection wall.

"What do you do for work?" I asked.

"Medical coding for insurance companies. It allows me to work from home and have flexible hours, if I choose." She cracked a smile at that.

"Flexible hours and working from home sound nice." I mirrored her smile, widening mine in encouragement. Hers dropped in response.

Great.

"Anything unusual happen in the time leading up to your husband's hospitalization?"

She shook her head, and turned to stare at the woman on the next-door porch. Neither acknowledged the other. Another nearly imperceptible sigh. "Why don't you come in? No need to put on a show for the neighbors."

"If you're sure?"

She turned without answering, opened the front door, and entered the house. Her beige slippers made a soft noise while she crossed her space. I followed, closing the door behind me.

Helen and her husband had filled their bright home with shades of blue in the décor, furniture accents, and crown molding. A slight citrus scent tickled my nose; an extinguished candle or air freshener, perhaps. On a bookcase, she or Alan had crammed an interesting assortment of knick-knacks, including jade stones, marine-life wood carvings, and an orange candle whose wax appeared to melt red.

A painting opposite the television dominated the space. Its striking appearance showed a woman made of flames on a sea blue background. Her arms were outstretched – in victory? I belatedly noticed Helen had perched on the edge of a white wicker chair, indicating I should sit on the covered couch. She crossed her legs and placed her hands in her lap, the image almost prim, despite the jeans and long-sleeved red knit top she wore.

I set my notebook on my knee and continued. "What happened on the day he first noticed any symptoms?"

"It was a normal day—" She stopped.

"Was it not a normal day?"

Helen shrugged. "The day he developed the fever, we'd had breakfast like usual, but then I went hiking while he was at work. We ran through this with the doctor, in case I'd been exposed to something that I then exposed my husband to." Her irritation flickered again.

"I appreciate you taking the time to review it with me," I said in a soft tone, barely managing not to snap at her. I reminded myself the emotion belonged to Helen. Her continued use of *my husband* rather than his name interested me. Grief? Or something else? "Was it a day off for you, that you could go hiking instead of working?"

Her nostrils flared. "No. I wanted to spend some time outside, so I shifted some of my work to another day."

"Oh, right, the flex hours." The impact of her words hit me and my pen stilled above the page. "You said you went hiking?"

"Yes. I hiked Crater Rim Trail at Volcanoes National Park. I wanted to see the lava." She half-smiled as she savored the memory. "It wasn't supposed to be that active there, but I just knew if I kept hiking, I'd find it."

My mind churned with the information. Cameron had said his wife spent the day 'hiking at the park'. Volcanoes National Park? I'd want to confirm that; perhaps the doctors had been on the right track looking for a transmittable illness. If so, this was way outside of my areas of expertise. "How long did you hike?"

"A few hours. I arrived home before dinner. Although my husband was already there."

"Was that normal?"

"No."

Ugh, this was excruciating. "Did you ask him why he was home early?"

"No. I assumed he needed a break, too."

I tilted my head. My guess was that hers had not been a happy marriage. "What did he do?" I asked.

"Financial analyst for Hawaii National Bank. Did you have any other questions?" Despite asking the question, her tone said she preferred me to go.

Time to go big or go home. "How are you doing with Alan's death?"

Her eyes narrowed.

"Not trying to pry," I assured her. "Just checking in with how you're doing." And see if I could knock something loose with my bluntness.

"I hope you can help your client's friend," she said, "I do. But I don't care that my husband is dead."

My jaw dropped open.

She sneered at me, her anger now on full display physically and psychically. "He deserved to die."

My eyes narrowed and I bit back an angry retort, part of me tethered to the reminder that Helen owned this feeling, not me, yet also not wanting to interrupt her flow. This was unexpected. Both her confession, and how much her emotion battered me with only one stone removed from my wall. I could only imagine how overwhelming it would be for me if I lowered the barrier altogether.

"He deserved it because he was cheating on me."

Okay, that explained a few things.

"Cheaters get everything they deserve. The wives can't keep—" She cut herself off and I wondered about the meaning behind the half-sentence.

"The wives can't keep… what?"

Her jaw clenched. "Nothing. I misspoke."

"Misspoke? It sounded like a very definitive thought."

She ignored my combative tone. "You don't have a response to my husband cheating on me?" she asked instead.

"Sorry, I had no idea."

"Obviously."

My body ached to mirror her clenched jaw and balled fists. I withstood the internal barrage and remained quiet, though I was a bit distracted because her angry energy had shifted. Now I detected hostility, though it seemed unusual somehow. I couldn't figure it out, and I didn't want to ignore Helen. For the moment, I chalked it up to her heightened level of hurt.

"Your statement threw me off guard, to be honest," I said. "I can only imagine how upset you must have been when you found out."

"You know, I found out that morning."

"That morning?"

"The morning he got sick."

"Ah, okay."

"He was so stupid," she continued. "He thought I was in the shower. I'd started the water, then realized I wanted to ask him a question. He was already on the phone with *her* when I stepped out of the bathroom." Her eyes closed and her face softened, but her voice became hard. "I heard him making plans."

"Are you certain that was it?" I played devil's advocate.

She snorted. "He ended the call with 'I love you'."

"What did you do?" The level of anger she radiated made me guess she confronted him, so her answer surprised me.

"Nothing. I got back in the shower. After he left, I decided I needed to get out into nature while considering my options. I thought the awesome power of the volcano would be a good distraction."

"And was it?"

"Yes." Her furious expression startled and inflamed me.

I tamped down my flare of hostility by rubbing my free hand on the cotton couch cover, the softness soothing me. Her eyes flicked to the movement, but she made no comment. After a quick debate, I asked one more question. "Do you know the name of the woman?"

"I got it off his phone," she boasted.

"Do you mind sharing it with me?"

"Annalisa Webster."

CHAPTER EIGHT

"How did you not say anything when Helen dropped the bombshell that our latest victim was her husband's mistress?" Mandie asked, her face swaying in front of her laptop's camera, hazel eyes moving between me and Jeff.

"Because I am a professional," I said, wiggling my eyebrows. Mandie and Jeff chuckled.

"At least we've established that our cases may not be as unconnected as they first appeared," he said. Moved from the ICU to his own room, he looked vastly improved from the day before. The relief I felt when I walked in this morning was palpable. I even dropped my protection wall a little, which increased my sense of fatigue, but confirmed no return of the chest pain or pressure he had experienced earlier. I now sat in a chair beside the bed, my wall firmly back in place, while we conducted our team video chat.

Jeff and I both peered at Mandie's face on the screen of my cellphone. My tale of Helen's interview brought the team up to speed – well, except for Daniel, who was on a plane flying out.

"What other information did you get?" I directed the question to my phone.

"Nothing earth-shattering. There's only one Annalisa Webster in Hawaii, so our newest victim is definitely the mistress. Her death mirrored Alan Richards'. She reported difficulty cooling off, going to the hospital when she began experiencing nausea. Her temperature rose over the next week until she experienced terminal organ failure."

We remained silent for a moment, considering another lost life. I cleared my throat. "What was her timeline from symptom onset to death?" Since she died a day after Alan, I hazarded an educated guess. "Eleven days?"

Mandie's brown curls bounced as she nodded on screen. "That seems to be accurate. According to the sister's posts, at least."

"Which brings us back to the most likely scenario. That this is an unknown pathogen. Virus, bacteria, something like that. Nothing supernatural," I said. "Right?"

"It suggests a communicable illness, yes," Jeff agreed. "It would help if we had a connection between Cameron and Annalisa since he denied knowing Alan."

I shook my head. "I popped into Cameron's room before I came here—"

"How's he doing?" Jeff interrupted. "I'm going to call his sister after we're done meeting."

"Not good. His temperature is up another degree."

"What does that make it now?" Mandie asked.

"104." I grimaced, remembering the flood of fear and overwhelming physical symptoms when I opened myself up to Cameron's experiences during my visit. Phantom heat suffused me and I waved a hand in front of my face before catching myself. "Poor guy. They've got him hooked up to an IV of chilled fluids, plus a fan in the corner of the room. It's not working. He's terrified he's dying, which seems to be his current path—"

"I can't go to his sister with that," Jeff interrupted again.

"I hear you, but you asked how he was doing," I said. "He continues to look like he just finished an intense workout; because of the sweating, he alternates between extreme heat and shaking from chills. Plus, he's developed a constant headache, besides the aches and nausea that are still there, despite the broad-spectrum antibiotics they tried."

"Which could point to it *not* being a pathogen, right?" Mandie asked.

I raised my hands in an I-don't-know gesture. "Not necessarily."

"Which is why we're investigating," Jeff said with a wink. We laughed in response.

"Oh, that's what I was getting to," I continued. "When I visited with Cameron this morning, he denied knowing Annalisa. I removed a stone when I asked, and there was no change in his emotions," I added, "suggesting he was telling the truth."

Jeff closed his eyes. I was about to ask him if he needed to rest when they opened. "We have three identified victims. Alan Richards. Annalisa Webster. Cameron Helms. The former two were involved in an extramarital affair and died within 10-11 days of displaying symptoms. In the absence of anyone additional, this suggests they were ... infected ... first. Cameron appears to have no connection to either of them and is definitely behind them in terms of symptom appearance. There must be others." His head lowered closer to the screen. "Were you able to find more people, Mandie?"

"Your interview list already includes Cameron's wife," she began to answer.

"Who, Cameron says, has no symptoms," I interjected.

"I found two more, Kevin Christian and Lacie Roberts, again with no seeming connection to each other or our known victims. At least according to their online footprints," Mandie amended. "I'll text you their info."

"Perfect, thanks. That will triple my remaining list," I said with a dry laugh. I twirled my pen, thinking about our next steps. "Have you looked beyond Hawaii yet?"

"Great minds think alike," Mandie said. "I set the forager on a continental United States search. I'm pretty sure I've exhausted the Hawaiian market, so to speak, but I've not opened up to international. If we get no hits within the U.S., I'll increase the radius again. The wider I go, the longer it will take to find results," she warned.

"Then nothing we've learned changes our approach," I concluded. "I'll double-check with Dr. Wilhelm that he still hasn't found evidence of a pathogen. For now, I'll continue with the interviews."

"Who's up next?" Jeff asked.

"Paula Helms. Cameron's wife."

CHAPTER NINE

The woman who answered the door of the cute art deco-style beach cottage at the end of the cul-de-sac had to be six feet tall – I'd only seen Cameron in his hospital bed. Was he this tall? And what was with all the tall people connected to this case? I stuffed a chuckle and smiled at the woman in the open door.

"May I help you?" Paula Helms tilted her head, considering me as I considered her, though I kept my protection wall raised for now. She wore an understated navy-blue wrap dress that emphasized her hourglass figure and highlighted her green eyes, which were also lightly lined in kohl. Her smattering of freckles across her nose and cheeks lent her a youthful air, despite being, most likely, in her thirties like her husband.

"Good morning. Are you Paula Helms?"

"Yes…"

"I'm Sarah Danger, a consultant on your husband's case." Her brow furrowed and I rushed to continue. "I work with the investigative team that Cameron's sister hired, from the mainland."

Paula's expression relaxed and she stepped aside to invite me in, her height dwarfing mine. I followed her through an elegant foyer to an airy living room. Bright white furniture with rainbow-colored accents made the smaller space feel larger. She passed through the room to the kitchen, which was spotless. We sat at an oak table in the breakfast nook. The white cabinets and gray quartz countertops contrasted well with the primary colors in the rather chaotic backsplash.

"How can I help you?"

"Since we didn't see you at the hospital—" The muscles tightened around her eyes. Interesting. "—we appreciate you seeing me in your home without notice. Right now, we're trying to get a sense of the timeline for the illness, as well as all the people who may have been impacted."

Paula's jaw dropped. "Do you think it's contagious? Am I at risk?"

"Sorry to have spooked you. If I had to make an educated guess, though I'm not a doctor, I would say if you haven't developed any symptoms yet, you're probably okay," I assured her.

"That's good." She pinned me with her gaze. "What questions do you have for me?"

"Take me through your routine leading up to Cameron's first reported symptoms."

Paula began a recitation of her everyday life. She drove back and forth to her job in Hilo as a copywriter for a media relations company. Her office catered lunch one of the days, and otherwise, she brought her own food.

Until she said, "When I realized how much leave I still had that wouldn't carry over to next year, I decided to take one day a week off to do something fun. That week, I hiked in the park. Like others, I was curious about the increased activity of the volcano."

"Kīlauea?"

"Yes, Kīlauea. Though with the restrictions," she said with a small shrug, "I didn't stay on any official path."

Cameron had said his wife went hiking the day he first noticed his symptoms. Now that she confirmed it, that meant we had at least two women who hiked at the volcano and may have returned with something else. Since the doctor reported all the testing came back clean, a supernatural explanation was looking more likely. Or could it still just be an undiscovered pathogen?

"What's wrong?"

My face must have telegraphed my consternation. I smiled and shook my head. "Thinking about the timelines, and trying to figure out how two unconnected men wound up infected with the same... issue."

Paula shrugged again, and a wave of negative energy lapped at the edges of my wall. Huh. I couldn't identify the energy, but it was off somehow. I smiled wider as I removed a stone to allow me to probe at the negativity while asking further questions.

"Just to tie up loose ends. Cameron said he didn't know Alan or Helen Richards. Do you?"

Paula shook her head.

"How about Annalisa Webster, Kevin Christian, or Lacie Roberts?"

"Are all of those people sick with the same thing my husband has?" Her hand fluttered to her face and a sudden need to flee to safety made my pulse jackrabbit.

The *off* energy intensified right before I replaced the stone in my protection wall, and it hit me that Paula's body language seemed forced. It might be worry over her husband, except that didn't feel accurate. How much time did she really spend at the hospital before Cameron insisted she go home and get some rest? Unable to identify what I was missing, I returned to my questioning. "Do you know any of those names?"

"I don't, sorry. What do you think that means? Do any of them know each other?"

"Actually, yes. The two we confirmed were acquainted were Alan Richards and Annalisa Webster." I hoped I wasn't speaking out of school to disclose something personal, but we needed a break in this case. "They were having an affair." The pure rage emanating off Paula at my comment was enough to threaten my barrier, though her face gave no sign.

"Interesting. And the others?" Her bland tone belied the still high level of anger flowing from her.

I needed a way past her defenses to what she was hiding. "We don't know yet. Does that mean anything to you?"

She dropped her hands to her lap. "Cameron was having an affair, too," she whispered.

And there it was. "Not with one of the people I listed, surely."

"No, not one of them. But when you said two of those people were cheating." The anger dipped as her eyes filled with tears that she rapidly blinked away. "I went hiking that day to clear my head and think about what I wanted to do."

"You just found out." A statement, not a question.

Her curt nod confirmed it. Hmm. Just like Helen Richards.

"Do you know the name of the woman?" I couldn't imagine how cheating tied into the spread of this illness. It seemed like another indicator of a supernatural origin for the fever. If it were an unknown pathogen, simple proximity would suggest that Paula and Helen would have caught it. And they didn't.

"Patricia Elliott. Someone Cameron worked with at the bank."

"Do you mind if I ask Cameron about her?"

Paula's breathing quickened at my question. She gave another curt nod.

"Do you mind if I speak to Patricia?" Technically speaking, I didn't need permission, but no reason to alienate the client's brother's wife.

"I want to know what's going on as much as you do. I'm not ready to give up on my marriage." Her jaw clenched, though maybe with determination instead of anger.

"Thank you." That having wrapped up my questions, we exchanged conversational pleasantries – nope, that wasn't a bit forced – and then I left her home. When the door behind me closed, I whipped out my phone and was back in the SUV by the time the hospital operator connected me to Cameron's room.

"I spoke to Paula this morning."

"How did that go? Did you learn anything helpful?" Was that an undercurrent of concern, or was I imagining it because of my newfound knowledge? I needed physical proximity for my clairempathy, so on the phone I had to rely on verbal inflection like everyone else.

"I'm not sure yet if it's helpful. It was interesting."

"What is it?"

"Do you know a Patricia Elliott?"

Cameron's loud silence on the other end told me everything.

CHAPTER TEN

Mandie sent me Patricia Elliott's address in response to my update text to her and Jeff. I'd decided to interview Patricia next since she had a connection to one of our victims. But the universe apparently had other plans and my call went straight to voicemail. Not to be stymied, I called Kevin Christian and Lacie Roberts. After all, they also lived in Hilo.

"Argh," I muttered at my phone after the third call went to voicemail. I chose not to leave any messages. This seemed best discussed in person. Rather than potentially waste a drive to Hilo, my curiosity got the best of me and I decided a visit to Volcanoes National Park was in order. Two women connected to this mystery had hiked the unexpectedly active volcano recently. I wanted to see or, more accurately, feel whatever there might be to feel.

After a short drive along Hawaii 11 from Mountain Eden, I reached the entrance to Volcanoes National Park. I turned off the road and approached the triangle-roofed hut housing the volunteer who would take my fee. The pass was good for a week, justifying the steep cost. It would at least cover any return trips.

Once inside the park, I headed straight for the Kīlauea Visitor Center. The single-story wooden structure ran the length of the parking lot. A United States flag rippled in the breeze. A handful of tourists stared at maps, deciding what they wanted to accomplish first. As I recalled from the online maps, if I was the one on vacation, I'd want at least a week to hike the trails.

I entered the building and approached Information. Large, colorful maps of the park covered the walls behind the two people standing at the desk.

"Welcome to the park." The smiling woman who greeted me wore a name tag on her tan button-down shirt identifying her as Ranger Cassidy. Next to her stood another woman, this one wearing a brown overcoat with patches signifying her as a volunteer.

"Thank you." I returned her smile uncertainly. "I have an unusual request, maybe."

"We'll do our best to assist you," Ranger Cassidy assured me, nodding her head, the halo of her black curly hair bouncing.

"I'd like to speak with a volcanologist, but understand the observatory isn't open because of the increased volcanic activity?"

The volunteer answered this question, running a hand through her short gray hair. "It's not as unusual a request as you might think. Lots of people would like to speak with a volcanologist when they visit. Especially right now."

"And, unfortunately, you are correct that nobody is available today," Ranger Cassidy added.

I thought a moment. "Can I schedule an appointment for another date?"

The ranger shook her head. "I'm afraid not. We aren't in a position to make appointments for the scientists."

"Is there someone else who can?"

"Normally, yes, but with the observatory closed—" The volunteer ended her statement with a sorrowful shrug.

Hmm. Now what?

"Doctor Sheri will be here tomorrow, though," Ranger Cassidy said. "She loves meeting with people, and is probably the most flexible with her time. We can't schedule anything, but if you come in the morning, you might have better luck."

"Thank you so much," I enthused, smiling wide. "And I'll take a map of the park, please."

Armed with my map, and making a note to explore the rest of what the center had to offer tomorrow, I headed back to the SUV. Knowing I was about to hike into off-limits territory, I also knew enough to alert my team to what I was doing. Just in case. Jeff texted back immediately.

Don't hike alone. It's unsafe.

I wanted to roll my eyes, but truthfully, I understood he was worried. And not really about the regular dangers.

We didn't know the role the volcano was playing in any of this, so my gift might leave me open to other unexpected nastiness.

Did I go or not? Of course, I was going!

I'll update you after, and I promise I'll be careful.

I drove along Crater Rim Drive until a sign at the Steam Vents parking lot informed visitors that this was the last parking lot before the road closure. Sure enough, orange cones blocked the road at the lot entrance. I pulled in and parked in the fairly empty lot.

Steam was visible from the SUV, and I walked over to check out the vents before starting my sneaking around. Four wooden posts created a rectangle surrounding one vent. Two beams connected each of the posts at the top and midway points, preventing a wayward tourist from tumbling into it. Gentle steam rose in the middle. Posted signs explained that the steam resulted from water trickling through the rocks until it came into contact with the liquid rock beneath. A mild sulfur odor tickled my nose.

Quick steps moved me into the closed section, while still staying near Crater Rim Drive. I blew out a tensely held breath when I saw a sign for the Kīlauea Military Camp. It turned out that waiting for someone to yell at you to stop was stressful. Unfolding the map I'd received at the visitor center, I confirmed the next step and headed inward toward the caldera.

My eyes widened at the increasing cracks in the hardened earth mixing with the sinkholes in the softer sections. The trail was a fascinating mix of desert scrub brush and groupings of trees I'd have expected in a lush rainforest. The lack of birdsong surprised me.

I stumbled to a stop. Nobody was near me, yet energy probed at my protection barrier. My mind checked the stone wall for any gaps or weaknesses and then I loosened a single stone to open myself up to what was present.

Smoke filled my nostrils. I was uncertain if that was real or supernatural. Rage flowed through me. It ripped a howl from my throat. My heart beat in my ears, a steady thumping.

Why was I here? What did I want? I didn't belong.

A gasp escaped and I braced my hands on my thighs, head dangling. Several deep breaths calmed me. I isolated the rage and the questions elicited, surrounding them in a solid, bright bubble in my mind. Those weren't me. I could let those go.

But the experience rattled me. I still felt the thoughts and emotions swirling around me, like being caught in a maelstrom. Jeff was probably right. This might be too dangerous to do alone. Not sure to whom I was speaking, nevertheless, I spoke into the forest.

"It's okay. I'm leaving."

And, I did, quickly retracing my steps back to the SUV, noting with relief, the reduction in that alien feeling the further from the caldera I got. A quick text to the team let them know I was fine.

I wasn't at all sure what to make of my experience, but decided I needed to step things up significantly.

CHAPTER ELEVEN

Another call to Patricia Elliott went straight to voicemail. Refusing to admit defeat, I hopped on Hawaii Belt Road, aka Route 11, and headed toward Hilo. I'd either get lucky or I wouldn't. The thirty-minute drive to Patricia's waterfront condo gave me time to think about the status of our case.

Alan was having an affair with Annalisa, and they both sickened and died from a fever-illness. Cameron and Patricia were also cheating, and he, at least, was lying in a hospital bed boiling from within. Would she be the same? And what about Kevin Christian and Lacie Roberts? Who were they and how were they connected to the string of illnesses? Surely they weren't also involved in an affair.

Soon, I pulled into the parking lot of a four-story condo complex. Signs led me to visitor parking, where I sat for a moment taking in the beige building with teal accents tracing the bottom of each floor's series of patios. I unexpectedly shivered after exiting the SUV. The weather had to be in the mid-70s, but the overcast day and brisk wind combined to make it cold to me. I reminded myself that it was December, after all, and hurried to the entrance.

Patricia Elliott had a top-floor condo and, if I was oriented right, she had a corner unit with 180-degree views of the ocean. After lowering my barrier a smidge, I knocked on the door. My smile faltered when a man answered. His brown eyes registered confusion and fatigue in an unlined face beneath buzz-cut brown hair.

"Yes?" He asked when I didn't identify myself.

"Of course, sorry," I sputtered. "I'm looking for Patricia Elliott?"

"She isn't feeling well. Would you like to leave a message?"

"I'm sorry to hear she isn't feeling well." I started with sympathy while I wracked my brain regarding how to handle this now. The guy before me might be Patricia's husband, unaware of her affair with Cameron. "Pardon my intrusion. Can you tell me what she's ill with?" A little lame without an explanation.

Untrusting energy spiked from the man in the door and I narrowed my eyes in response. He pushed up the long sleeves of his blue pullover and shoved his hands into the pockets of his jeans. "Why would you want to know that?"

Why would I want to know? I cleared my throat. "I'm not at liberty to disclose the exact nature of my inquiry –

client confidentiality – but my team's investigating an unusual illness that has infected several people on the Big Island."

He tilted his head. "What type of illness?"

"Fever-based."

He pulled his hand out of his pocket and extended it to me. "Russell Chase. Patty is my girlfriend. I think you'd better come in."

His energy was more trusting now, and consequently, my trust in him swelled. I shook his hand and followed him into the condo. And confirmed my earlier guess. The unit had amazing views from floor-to-ceiling windows overlooking a balcony and the panoramic scenery beyond. Some type of dense green plant surrounded a smattering of pine trees that extended perhaps fifty feet from the building. These ended at a black rocky beach and the ocean. The endless horizon stretched before us. I idly wondered about the cost; a similar view in one of the coastal areas surrounding Tampa would be prohibitively expensive. The condo itself appeared in decent condition, if a bit dated. I imagined they didn't care all that much; you bought a place like this for that view.

We sat on opposite ends of an L-shaped blue cloth couch, moving aside several throw pillows to do so. My head swiveled, looking for Patricia. The air hung heavy in the room, the higher humidity at the coast evident in the closed-up condo.

"Patty's in the bedroom," Russell answered my unasked question. "Probably sleeping."

"Am I right to assume she has a fever?"

"For several days now. I've tried acetaminophen and ibuprofen; neither worked. She's staying hydrated, though stopped eating this morning, from the nausea."

I didn't need my clairempathy to catch the worry in his words. "I'm not sure how much it will help, but let me tell you what I can." Without including names, I explained about the illness progression. Russell blanched when I reached the part about people dying.

"Should I take Patty to the hospital?"

What could I say – it hasn't mattered so far? Instead, I said, "It couldn't hurt. Perhaps you could get some of her things together in an overnight bag while I speak with her. If she's awake," I hurried to add.

"That's a good idea." He stood and I scrambled to follow. "Wait. Why did you come to check on her?"

"Um."

He crossed his arms over his chest, appearing quite intimidating for a man of average height and weight.

"I can't disclose that without disclosing the identity of our client."

One corner of his upper lip rose in a sneer. "That's convenient."

"It's not a matter of convenience." I held eye contact and opened my palms, silently asking him to trust me.

He deflated. "I guess it doesn't matter."

I followed him to a closed door. We heard a muffled response to his gentle knock, and took that as permission to enter.

Patricia Elliott looked bad. As bad as Cameron, if not worse. Her nifty rainbow-colored hair was plastered to her head from sweat, which was not quite pouring down the sides of her face, as if in a cartoon. A thin body lay on top of the covers, one arm over her stomach and the other curled against her side. Her blue eyes appeared glassy. I didn't know if that was from the fever, nausea, or some other pain.

"What was her temperature the last time you took it?" I whispered to Russell.

"105 an hour ago." He strode toward her, sat on the queen-sized bed, and cradled one of her hands in his. "Patty, honey, there's a woman here to speak with you. Do you feel up to it?"

She faced him, paused a moment, then licked her lips. "Okay. Who is she?"

I stepped further into the room. "My name is Sarah Danger. I'm a consultant on a case regarding an unexplained fever-illness that has stricken several people."

Patricia nodded. "I'm not sure how I can help, but I'll try." Her voice sounded gravelly like she hadn't had water in days.

I glanced between her and Russell. He stood from the bed and moved to the closet to put together a bag of clothes, as I'd suggested, except that kept him in the room. How could I ask my questions with him present? I started with softballs, taking her through her illness progression like I had with Cameron. Her symptoms lined up with his, in terms of manifestation and timeline, although if I remembered correctly, his temperature today was a degree less than hers.

Now the tricky part. "We're trying to determine how the illness is spreading so we can narrow down the source."

Patricia nodded in understanding.

"I'm going to list some names. Tell me if you know any of them."

Another nod of understanding. Russell had stopped filling the bag and turned to watch the scene unfold.

"Alan Richards?" Negative shake of the head. "Annalisa Webster?" Head shake. "Kevin Christian?" Head shake. "Lacie Roberts?" Head shake. I kept my voice in the same tone and inflection with the final name. "Cameron Helms?" Minute pause and then stronger head shake. The anxiety spike off of Patricia would have confirmed her lie, even if her body language hadn't.

"Are you sure?" I asked.

"Of course, I'm sure," she snapped.

I glanced again between her and Russell.

"It's just that... we heard word to the contrary."

"I don't know what you heard. They're mistaken. I don't know anybody on that list." Her eyes pleaded with me to stop, and misery flared in me from both Patricia and myself. I hated causing her this pain.

Now Russell looked back and forth between me and his girlfriend. "What's going on, honey? Why would somebody say you know someone that you don't?"

"I don't know. I don't know any of those people," she insisted, but her voice trailed off.

"Two of the people on that list have died." I grimaced. "If there's an angle we can't explore, more deaths may result." I tried for matter-of-fact. Still, she gasped.

"I…" Her gaze ricocheted between her boyfriend and me.

"Please, Patricia," I pleaded.

"Cameron Helms," she said in a rush. "I used to work with him at the bank."

"Why would that be a big deal?" Russell asked, confused by her earlier reticence.

She looked at me and I jumped in, hoping we could skirt the issue. I'd found the connection; I only needed one more piece of information. "When was the last time you saw him?"

"Last week."

"Before you were ill?" I asked.

"Yes."

"Okay," I said, naively thinking we'd get through this unscathed. "That's all I needed; to find a connection to someone who's become ill. I'll see myself out," I continued over Russell's attempt to speak, and directed my words his way. "I'll leave my card on your kitchen counter; please tell me if she's admitted to the hospital. You can also call for updates on the case. I can share what's not confidential." I took two steps back toward the door.

"Why didn't you want to admit you knew this Cameron?" Russell asked his girlfriend. He had retaken his seat on the side of the bed, but had not retaken Patricia's hand, and his posture was rigid.

Her mouth opened and closed like a fish.

"It's not a complicated question." He stood and stepped away from her. Coldness had seeped into his tone. I wondered if he'd suspected something before my visit.

"I don't know," she finally rasped. Her left hand flopped up in a half-hearted gesture.

"You don't know? That's convenient," he responded, his words echoing those he'd said to me earlier.

"He was just someone I worked with," she insisted. "I didn't think about it."

Russell barked a laugh. "You didn't think about it?"

"I'll see myself out," I repeated, interrupting the uncomfortable conversation.

"Please do me the courtesy of telling me the truth," Russell said in a low voice.

"I…" A single tear escaped, mingling with the sweat on her face. "There's nothing to tell," she insisted. "We're friends. Not even friends," she corrected herself. "Just friendly."

Methinks the lady doth protest too much. It didn't take a clairempath to know something was amiss.

Hurt mushroomed within Russell at her explanation and I wanted to cry. He turned to me with a veiled expression. "I agree. I think you should leave. Thank you for the information about how the others have done and are doing. I'll get Patricia to the hospital."

I didn't miss his reversion to using her full name. She sobbed now, her hand reaching for him to come back to her. Hurt continued to radiate off of Russell, but no malice.

I believed he would take her to the emergency room as promised. The details of their relationship weren't relevant to the case, as far as I could tell, so I backed to the door of the bedroom. I opened my mouth to – what, apologize for trying to expose her dirty laundry? Instead, I fled the condo, pausing to fumble a card out of my pocket, no longer noticing the incredible view.

CHAPTER TWELVE

Where was our case? Two women being cheated on who hiked the unexpectedly active volcano, whose husbands and their lovers became sick. This could suggest passing some kind of pathogen, except the wives themselves weren't ill. Unless it was mere coincidence that they were just carriers, I'd bet my not-yet-earned doctoral degree that something supernatural was in play, especially given my unsettling experience hiking near the volcano.

Before I figured out the cause, I decided I wanted a bit more evidence to support my odd theory. After all, once is chance, two may still be a coincidence, but three is a pattern. I needed to speak to Kevin Christian and Lacie Roberts. Kevin was married and Lacie was not. Hmm. I turned the key in the ignition and lowered the windows to get some ventilation while I debated who to visit first.

An idea struck. I switched the SUV back off, grabbed my phone from the center console, and entered Lacie's number. A hoarse voice carried over the line.

"Hello?"

"Hi, my name is Sarah Danger. May I speak to Lacie Roberts, please?"

"This is she."

"I'm not at liberty to disclose the exact nature of my interest – client confidentiality – but my team is investigating an unusual sickness that has infected several people on the Big Island. And it has come to my team's attention that you might have this fever-illness." Almost word for word what I'd used with Russell Chase, and the businesslike efficiency worked with him. Drumming my fingers on my thigh, I waited for her reaction. The silence stretched on to the point I thought we'd been disconnected.

"How do you know I'm sick?"

Her accusatory question wasn't off the mark, so I tried for a piece of the truth Mandie had provided from her research. "Your sister."

A soft sigh. "Oh, of course. She's really worried."

"May I ask you a few questions?"

"If you think it could help."

"I do," I assured her. Now for the tricky part. "Would you mind if I conferenced in another person? That way I can compare your experiences. I'll only use first names, to protect your privacy. He's also ill," I added as an afterthought, hoping to play on her desire to help.

"Um, okay?"

She was definitely confused, and perhaps her sick state made her more susceptible to agreeing to a plan that on the surface made zero sense. I ran with it before she thought too hard about what I was asking. "Thank you so much. I'll be right back with the other person." I placed her on hold and entered the number for Kevin Christian.

When he answered, sounding hoarse and tired as well, I had a replay of the introductory conversation with Lacie, even down to the confusion about joining a conference call. But he too said yes. My heart hammering in my chest about what I was setting into motion, I merged the two calls.

"Let me start by thanking you both for agreeing to speak with me together," I began.

The couple murmured, "You're welcome."

"As I explained, this will allow me to compare your experiences." Time to drop the first bomb. "For privacy purposes, I'm only going to refer to you by your given names. Kevin, meet Lacie. Lacie, meet Kevin." The smell of unidentifiable spicy food wafted through the open windows of the SUV. I sniffed at the air during the extra beat of silence that greeted my introduction.

"Um, hi?" Kevin at last said. "Lacie?"

"Hi Kevin," she whispered.

"Do you two know each other?" I asked.

"Of course not," he responded quickly to my feigned shock. Lacie didn't respond.

"Oh, because the way you both said hi, it kind of sounded like you did."

"How would we know each other?" His question held an unspoken challenge.

"It's not that big of an island," I sidestepped.

"Who are you? Who hired you?" Kevin demanded.

Okay, one more push should do it. "Why are you upset, Kevin, if the two of you don't know each other?"

"Lacie, what's going on?" He slipped and asked.

"I don't know," she answered, but I smiled at his mistake.

"That's an interesting question for a perfect stranger," I commented. When I then heard subdued crying, guilt blossomed over my glee in correctly guessing their relationship. "Lacie, I'm sorry. I wasn't trying to ambush you."

"Who are you? How did you know we knew each other?" Lacie asked.

"Educated guess." I explained about the two dead lovers, the two sick lovers, and the wives who hiked the volcano. "I haven't identified the connection, yet. It seemed reasonable that you two might be... involved."

Kevin snorted. "First of all, I'm married. And, second of all, what on earth could hiking have..." His voice trailed off.

"What is it?" I asked.

"Natalie – that's my wife – she hiked that volcano recently too. I don't remember the exact day. It was before Lacie and I got sick."

"Are we going to die?" Lacie asked, fear coating each word.

"I would suggest you both head to the hospital," I evaded her question. What could I say? It didn't look good? I never questioned them about their symptoms, but neither of them sounded healthy. "Tell them about the prior deaths in Mountain Eden, in case they aren't aware. I'm sure they'll admit you, so they can do everything possible while we search for the cause."

"I don't understand how this is happening," Kevin said, bewildered.

"I don't either," I admitted. "But thank you both for telling me the truth, which at least confirms we have a pattern."

"I guess," he responded, his voice now despondent. "Will you have to tell my wife?"

"I will want to speak with her, yes, to ask about her hike." Time for some major honesty. "It would be better if you told her first."

"Confession is good for the soul," he bit out.

Lacie's sobbing intensified.

"I don't know about all that. It has to be preferable to hear it from you than from me. It wouldn't be my intention to disclose it, but if your wife isn't a complete idiot, she'd likely figure it out by my questions. Besides," I added, trying to be gentle, "it's always possible she already knows."

His sharp inhalation suggested he hadn't considered that possibility. "I'll talk with her about going to the hospital, and about Lacie." He stumbled on her name. "Maybe meet us there?"

"Hilo Medical Center?" I confirmed. An ambulance siren carried on the wind through my open window, and I glanced in the general direction of the sound.

"Yes," he answered.

"That's where I'm heading too," Lacie said, in a small voice. "I'll let you decide whether to acknowledge me if we see each other."

My heart broke for her. Kevin's question about his wife didn't shock her, so she knew he was married. It still had to hurt to expect you'd be ignored by someone you care for. This whole case made me glad I'd chosen to stay single.

CHAPTER THIRTEEN

The lovely woman at the Information desk inside the lobby of the three-story shades-of-beige Hilo Medical Center directed me to the emergency department. A short walk down the righthand hallway found me in another beige room with darker neutral carpeting and sliding glass doors opposite, which appeared to be the proper emergency entrance. The silence struck me first. Besides the shifting of bodies in the rows of yellow-green vinyl chairs, nobody spoke, not even whispered conversations between individuals who'd arrived together.

However. The energy pouring off the dozen people scattered across the room, seated, slouched, slumped over the sides of the chairs, overcame my stone protection barrier and nearly knocked me backward. I needed to isolate and separate them from my own; this wasn't something I normally had to do. Avoidance normally did the trick. But this made twice on this trip. Closing my eyes, I stepped closer to the wall, out of the way of any other people, and focused on the swirl. First, I pictured a peaceful, white bubble. With it secure in my mind, I wrapped the emotions in my bubble and attempted to match them to individuals' body language to identify Kevin, his wife Natalie, and Lacie, and release the rest. Sweat beaded on my forehead. Maybe I should have asked Mandie to text pictures of the three.

There. I found them.

A couple sat stiffly next to each other, with another woman a few seats down. All three appeared to be in their forties and fit. The women bore an uncanny resemblance to each other, with their short blond hair, brown eyes, and no makeup. The man had light brown hair that was graying at his temples, his brown eyes directed, unfocused, at the floor. They each tried to surreptitiously appraise the others. Pinched expressions and sweat dripping off flushed faces identified the two who were sick. Hurt and fear gushed off them. I chanced removing a single stone from my protection wall for the briefest of moments, and the resulting onslaught confirmed their emotions were directed at each other, as opposed to an amorphous fear of an illness. All stared at me when I approached, still catching my breath and calming my heart rate.

"Kevin and Natalie Christian?" Starting with them made the most sense. They could decide if they wanted to include Lacie in this initial discussion.

They nodded, confused. "Are you with the hospital?" Natalie asked.

I glanced down at myself as if to confirm I was wearing the jeans and short-sleeved blouse I remembered donning this morning, and not scrubs. After I introduced myself, understanding dawned in Kevin's eyes but confusion deepened in Natalie's.

"You're not with the hospital. You're a consultant hired by the family member of a person who became ill with something similar to Kevin," Natalie parroted back what I'd said.

I looked to Kevin before continuing and he gave a slight nod. This tacit permission provided, I launched into the explanation I'd given Kevin and Lacie on the phone. Natalie paled when I got to the part about cheated-on women hiking at the volcano park, though she stayed silent. I turned at the sound of light footsteps behind me.

"Kevin Christian?" A soft-spoken woman wearing scrubs asked the question. When Kevin nodded, she asked him to follow her. Natalie mutely rose to follow. Another nurse approached Lacie and took her away for evaluation.

Well, that wasn't very successful. I double-checked my protection barrier was at full strength to block the remaining people in the waiting room before taking a seat myself. I hoped the hospital would admit both Kevin and Lacie, for observation at a minimum, and I'd check in with them after.

While time ticked by, I scanned social media to see if anything exciting was happening in the world. My jaw dropped when I saw a post from Catherine Rodham. She and I had met in a social media group for psychics, of all places. I'd joined with little expectation, to be honest, expecting most people to be confused, delusional, or con artists. And I was wrong.

Catherine's post said she was in Hawaii, on her honeymoon, so I sent her a quick message, to see if we could meet up while I was here. She lived in Las Vegas, running the west coast arm of what had become known as the Paranormal Talent Agency. The volume of energy in Vegas would no doubt have me cowering. I couldn't imagine my protective wall providing much relief, certainly not if I went anywhere near the Strip.

Message sent, I debated if I should find the cafeteria for a quick bite. Then Natalie surprised me by hurrying through the doors she'd gone through twenty minutes prior.

I rose to meet her. She held out her hands as if needing comfort, but withdrew them. A slight earthy scent surrounded her. Sandalwood, perhaps. She sat in a chair, so I retook my own. I waited for her to begin.

"When Kevin mentioned the couple who died, the doctor started the admissions process." Her voice shook and her eyes welled with tears. "Since the second couple got sick, the emergency doctors have kept an eye out for more... victims?"

Heartened as I was by this acknowledgment that there was a real problem, it still didn't get me any closer to figuring out what was going on.

"I wanted to talk to you before he got moved to his room," Natalie continued. "You probably already guessed, but I went hiking at Volcanoes National Park the day Kevin first said he didn't feel well."

"Kīlauea?"

She nodded. "I'm fascinated by the volcano's extra activity."

"So, you weren't there for," I struggled to find the right word, "stress relief?"

She snorted. "You're asking if I knew he was cheating?"

Now I nodded.

"Yes, I did, and yes, I was considering my options while I hiked. We'd drifted apart," she admitted. "I figured it was normal ups and downs for a married couple. Until I found out about her."

"How long have you been married?"

"Fifteen years." She frowned. "I don't know what to do. I don't want to lose him."

Her palpable grief highlighted what I realized had been missing – anger. Even after removing a stone from my barrier, what flowed in contained no anger. She didn't seem angry at her husband for cheating. "You're not mad?"

"I'm not happy," she said with a shrug. "But it takes two to ruin a relationship. I could have been more proactive."

"You don't think he deserved to get sick?" I asked, remembering Helen Richards' comment about her husband, Alan.

Natalie's eyes widened and she shook her head. "No, of course not." She thought a moment. "I believe we can survive this. But if he wants to leave me, he should. Life is too short not to be happy."

"That is a remarkable attitude," I responded, unsure I'd be able to feel the same way if I'd found myself in her situation. Hah. The overwhelming need to yell, *this is bull*, rose up. Wait. Was that me or her? An energy shift drew my attention then receded as fast. I replaced my stone and realized she had continued speaking.

"I asked the doctor if I could have picked up a virus or bacteria at the volcano that then infected Kevin. The doctor blew me off, said there's nothing to suggest that." Anger tinged her voice now.

I sighed. "Yeah, my contact at Mountain Eden Hospital ran almost every test imaginable, even sending samples to the CDC for more in-depth tests, and so far, nothing."

"Is there anything we can do?" She watched me with such expectation, I wanted to hide from the scrutiny.

"I don't think so."

Natalie rose from the chair and I scrambled to follow. "They expect to get him assigned to a room within the hour. If there's nothing else, I'll head back there." She grasped my hands in her own. "Please let us know if you find out anything."

"I will." I watched her walk through the doors to the patient care area before retaking my seat, propping my right elbow on the thin armrest.

The information we'd learned suggested two radically different theories, neither of which we had concrete evidence to support.

Theory #1: Somehow, in a thus-far undetectable way, hikers at Kīlauea were becoming carriers of a virus or bacterium they passed to their partners, who passed it to their lovers.

Theory #2: Somehow, in a thus-far unexplainable way, cheated-on women were infecting their partners with a supernatural illness that they passed on to their lovers.

I wasn't a doctor, so I'd leave that avenue to Dr. Wilhelm and his ilk. Nor was I a volcano expert, further limiting my ability to help confirm or eliminate the first theory. But at least I knew where I might find such an expert, who could speak to whether or not it was even possible for a volcano to carry illnesses.

CHAPTER FOURTEEN

"Good morning," I called out to the most recent addition to our team. Daniel Trawl appeared awfully alert for having flown from Tampa to Hilo late last night. The benefit of being in his early twenties, I supposed. Dan looked like he stepped out of the pages of a hiking magazine. He wore tan hiking pants, brown leather hiking boots, and a deep-green long-sleeved shirt that made his hazel eyes pop from behind frameless glasses. No doubt the shirt had SPF built-in and was moisture-wicking.

"Good morning, doc," he replied.

"Not yet," I said by rote as he walked to the SUV from our vacation rental. He was staying in Jeff's apartment at the moment; it seemed easier than getting him a separate place when we'd already paid for Jeff's.

"Time to hike?"

I'd emailed him a summary of the investigation's status and my plan for visiting Volcanoes National Park. We had strong evidence that hiking near the volcano was related to the illness, given the three women hiking it and their connection to those who were ill. Not to mention my own experience yesterday. The goal today: put a final nail in the coffin, so to speak, of an actual pathogen causing the fever-illness. Doctor Wilhelm previously stated all his tests had come back normal; this morning he confirmed the CDC hadn't found anything either. When I'd expressed surprise at how quickly they'd run their tests, he'd sent a laughing emoji, along with "What can I say, I know a guy."

Thus, much like a mental health counselor wanted physical explanations eliminated before considering psychiatric diagnoses, I was ready to completely eliminate any physical cause before investigating supernatural ones. The final nail in that coffin would be confirming that volcanoes can't harbor viruses or bacteria that could cause what was happening. The internet said they couldn't, but you can't believe everything you read on the internet, right? And, not that I had a supernatural cause to consider. Although something had been percolating at the back of my mind since I interviewed Helen Richards, our first victim's wife. I just couldn't quite catch hold of it yet.

"Yes," I said, brimming with excitement about hiking the volcano again. This time I'd be able to go farther. I also hoped we'd have better luck speaking with a volcanologist. My outfit, not as stylish as Dan's, would be serviceable for today. Hiking pants and a dark-blue long-sleeved hoodie over a super stretchy nylon short-sleeved shirt. Although I didn't own hiking boots, I had some nice trail shoes. I'd wanted to wear shorts, to be honest, but the cloudiness from yesterday had continued and the temperature was stubbornly stuck in the high sixties. I lived in Tampa for a reason – anything under 70 degrees was too cold!

We hopped into the SUV and I repeated my steps from yesterday, ending in the parking lot for the Kīlauea Visitor Center. Dan and I entered the single-story building and headed straight for Information. We were in luck. Ranger Cassidy stood behind the desk, again wearing a tan button-down shirt and a big smile.

"You're back," she said.

"Yes, and I brought my teammate." I held up both hands, showing crossed fingers. "I'm hoping Doctor Sheri will be able to see us?"

The ranger's brown eyes twinkled and she reached for a walkie-talking. "Let me see what I can do." The ranger spoke into the walkie-talkie, explaining that some visitors wanted to speak with someone about the volcanoes. Did she have time to answer a few questions? The volcanologist confirmed her availability with the ranger, who resumed speaking to us. "Like I mentioned yesterday, Doctor Sheri loves talking to visitors; she doesn't always have time, but she tries."

We expressed our sincere thanks, gave her our names, and then followed the suggestion to have a look around until Doctor Sheri arrived at the visitor center. I was thrilled to have the opportunity to explore. Exhibits covered the walls of this primary room, discussing everything from the mechanics of island formation to the ecosystems present in the park. Not being familiar with Hawaiian history, I most enjoyed the stories, known as mo'olelo, of the Native Hawaiians interspersed throughout. It was fascinating to read their experiences and explanations for the creation of their world.

"Sarah?"

I pivoted toward the voice. "Yes?" My peripheral vision sighted Dan walking over.

A woman in her mid-thirties stood before me wearing an outfit almost identical to the one Dan wore. Her blond ponytail was pulled through the space above the back closure of her tan baseball cap. Her wide smile revealed a mild gap between her front teeth and she stuck out her hand in greeting.

"Doctor Sheri?" I confirmed. At her nod, I continued. "Thank you for agreeing to meet with us." We followed her lead when she stepped to a far corner, away from the few tourists milling around the visitor center. I succinctly outlined where we were. She was already shaking her head no before I got to my main question about a pathogen released by the volcano causing the fever-illness.

"Sorry to disappoint you," she said.

"I wouldn't say disappointment is the right emotion," I interjected with a small laugh. "I don't want the volcano to be making people sick."

"Fair enough," the volcanologist conceded. "I'm sorry that I can't offer an explanation," she amended. "But, there's virtually no way for the volcano to release an unknown pathogen."

"Haven't people sickened after volcanic eruptions in the past?" Dan asked.

"Of course," Doctor Sheri agreed. "But not for the reason you might be thinking. If you'll allow me a quick lesson?" When we nodded, she continued.

"It's the gases emitted during an eruption that can kill living beings, and not only humans. An eruption can emit different gases, including hydrogen sulfide and carbon dioxide, that, at least for the latter, many people are aware can be deadly. So, direct inhalation can do it. Also, though not as well known, if the area plants absorb gases like sulfur and chlorine, and then other organisms ingest the plants, that can kill those organisms too."

"Wow, that's wild," I responded, belatedly realizing I might want to take notes, and whipping my notepad out of my black backpack.

"And, of course, if sewage systems are damaged or crops are killed by lava or accompanying earthquakes, then famine and disease may follow. But they aren't a result of pathogens released from the volcano," she concluded. She lifted a finger. "That's not to say it couldn't happen, but volcanoes are considered self-sterilizing."

I closed my eyes in thought for a moment. "That makes perfect sense."

"Can we see the current eruption?" Dan asked.

"No, I'm sorry, only as a distant red glow," the volcanologist answered. "That area is closed. And, it might be best to skip even the open areas today. We're running some tests, so it'll be overrun with scientists."

Disappointment surged that we couldn't risk hiking today.

"The summit collapse has again made the overlook unsafe," Doctor Sheri continued. "Cracks and sinkholes have developed all over the area, including again damaging Crater Rim Drive."

"Again?" I asked, a vague recollection of Kīlauea erupting before surfacing in my mind.

"This isn't the first time Kīlauea has had an unusual eruption." Her lips pursed. "Though this one is different. A few years ago, a decades-long effusive eruption concluded with some intense activity. Pressure increasing below Puʻu ʻŌʻō spread through the system, and the lava lake at Halemaʻumaʻu rose to the point it overflowed onto the crater floor. The damage was extensive, not just to the park, but to the surrounding neighborhoods." She frowned. "Once the summit of Puʻu ʻŌʻō itself collapsed, the lava lake began to drop. That concluded the eruption cycle, then earthquakes followed for months after. We believed everything was finished, spent a couple of years repairing the damage. And then 16 days ago, it started erupting again, seeming like it might repeat." Her frown deepened. "Which made no sense."

"How come?" I asked, scribbling notes, including 16 DAYS in big block letters. Sixteen days lined up with when Helen Richards hiked the volcano and Alan developed the terminal fever.

"There have been no surface lava flows at Kīlauea since that major event."

"It's still an active volcano, right?"

"It is," she agreed. "But—"

We waited for her to gather her thoughts.

"Lava has begun flowing, and it's a bit more than effusive this go-'round. Except thus far there's been no magma system pressure increase or really any physical explanation for why the lava would flow like this."

"It's defying physics?" I asked with a nervous chuckle. That would be one tick in the supernatural column.

"I wouldn't quite say that. I would say that the rest of the readings appear inconsistent with the lava activity. And we haven't pinpointed the reason for the inconsistency." She lifted her arms in an I-don't-know gesture. "It's fascinating but unexplained at this point."

Dan and I thanked Doctor Sheri for her time, and she bid us good luck. We would need it, now that we felt confident that the cause of the illness wasn't physical. If the Hawaiian doctors, CDC, and park service PhDs couldn't find a physical explanation, there likely wasn't one. That left something or someone supernatural killing people. A chill ran down my spine at the thought, and I cursed my overactive imagination.

CHAPTER FIFTEEN

Dan and I arrived at the hospital in time to watch Jeff eat lunch: chicken tenders, mashed potatoes, and wiggling green jello. The baked chicken smelled surprisingly good, and my stomach rumbled. I'd need food soon, too.

"Do you remember Catherine Rodham?" I directed the question at Jeff while Dan worked to connect with Mandie via video chat.

"The lie-detector psychic?"

I snorted and Dan paused in his efforts. "That's the one," I confirmed. "She's in Hawaii on her honeymoon. Can you believe it? I scheduled drinks with her tonight to catch up. Figured I'd run our case by her, given her experience in the paranormal."

"Let us know if she has anything interesting to add," Jeff said.

"Will do."

Dan's eyes widened. "Am I invited?"

"Of course," I assured him.

Dan greeted Mandie in the video chat and then set his cellphone on the food tray. He leaned it against a carton of milk, so our heads looked tiny on massive upper bodies. But at least we were all visible to her.

I couldn't shake the feeling of unease I'd picked up during our conversation with Doctor Sheri. We needed to a direction to go in. We'd run out of people to interview and we were running out of time for Cameron, Patricia, Kevin, and Lacie. I summarized our findings from the morning.

"The area is closed because of the increasing and unexplained instability." I gave an impish smile. "So, we'll need to go around that to investigate. In the meantime, though, at least nobody else should be exposed."

"That explains why I haven't found any new cases," Mandie interjected. "No one can get close enough to whatever supernatural force is at play here."

"Are we comfortable calling it supernatural now?" Dan asked. He and I sat on chairs pulled to either side of Jeff's hospital bed.

"I would think so," Jeff answered, speaking around a mouthful of food.

"Me too," I concurred. "Our next step is to figure out the nature of the supernatural force."

"I'd say," Mandie's voice emerged from the phone and we focused on her, "there are two primary questions related to that step. The first is whether or not the source of the force is Helen, since it seems to have started with her, or the volcano itself. The second is whether or not the force is aware."

Dan whistled. "Is it possible someone or something could be causing this and have no idea?"

I nodded. "Absolutely. We've had cases like that before. This was before your time, Dan," I said, then glanced between Jeff and Mandie, "but I know you two remember the Egyptian curse in Pompano Beach. The owner of the pottery indeed had no idea the person who sold it to him had activated a curse."

Eyes wide, Dan blurted out, "That story would have been perfect for my new blog."

"New blog?" I quirked an eyebrow. When he first asked to shadow me as a volunteer, it had been in part for his existing blog.

Red tinged his cheeks. "It came to me on the plane. I'm rebranding and chronicling our more unique stories."

"I thought you were already chronicling the more interesting ones," I said. "Not that we've had many since you joined."

"Yes." He tapped his foot against the floor. "Not just interesting, though. The supernatural ones. The truly unique cases. Continuing to remove identifying information, of course," he hurried to add. He waggled his eyebrows at me. "Wanna be my first interview?"

I bit the inside of my cheek to not laugh aloud. "We'll talk about it later."

"What do you think?" Mandie asked, redirecting us like her children.

I smothered a smile. "I agree with the questions. Helen was angry enough when I spoke with her to be the source." Something niggled at the back of my mind, then retreated when I chased after it. "But she seemed as perplexed by what was going on as we are. My best guess is either she's not the source or, if she is, she's unaware."

"Since it appears to be connected to the volcano, at a minimum, perhaps it's tied to Hawaiian nature or culture?" Jeff surmised. The three of us nodded in agreement.

"Let's research Hawaii further," I declared. "We'll divide and conquer. Mandie, if you'll tackle natural phenomena, while Dan and I can tackle culture, including mythology." My voice trailed off, and I gripped the arms of the chair, the metal cool under my fingers, as things clicked in my mind.

The weird energy when I interviewed Helen Richards.

The Hawaiian décor, specifically the candle that burned red and the flame-woman painting.

A fever-based illness.

Dan and Jeff stared at me; even Mandie's face angled in my direction on the screen. I tapped my fingers together while I ran through the scenario.

"Give me one second to confirm this." I did a quick internet search on my cellphone. "Ah-ha!"

"Quit keeping us in suspense," Jeff demanded, but with a smile. The beeping of the machines connected to him stayed steady.

"I might have part of the answer." Before continuing, I told them what I remembered of Helen's home décor and the odd hostile energy that I couldn't quite pin down during Helen's interview. "The red flame woman could be Pele, the Goddess of Fire. And that energy could be related to whatever force is causing the—"

"Fever-illness!" Mandie shouted the rest of my sentence.

I pointed at her. "Exactly. Pele, of course, is a Hawaiian goddess of incredible power. But what the internet confirmed is that, besides being the goddess of volcanoes and fire, she's also the goddess of passion, jealousy, and capriciousness."

"In other words, she'd be the perfect goddess to strike down cheating partners," Jeff concluded. "Good work."

"If a goddess is responsible, how do we fix it?" Dan asked, bewildered.

"Not so fast," I said. "While this gives us a direction, we still don't have answers to those basic questions Mandie identified. They're only modified a little. Is the source of the force," I ticked them off on my fingers, "Helen, Pele, or the volcano itself? Is the force aware of what it's doing?"

"If I'm understanding correctly, we need to determine if Helen somehow 'woke' Pele or the volcano? Or, if Helen's hike to the volcano 'woke' her own powers?" Dan responded to my proposed questions with his own.

We pondered the implications. My heart raced at the immense power of Pele. I grinned. "Looks like tomorrow we're getting closer to that volcano."

CHAPTER SIXTEEN

Catherine Rodham and her new husband, Alex Moore, had chosen a beach vacation for their honeymoon, so of course, they were on the other side of the island in Kona. The ninety-minute drive passed without delay, however, and we arrived in time for happy hour.

And appetizers at least for me. I was starving. We snagged a parking spot – score! – and crossed the street to enter the Kona institution, Huggo's On the Rocks. I'd wondered about the unusual name, given that, according to the internet, the founder's name was Hugo... trying to be different? But I digressed.

Although the sun sat low on the horizon, its powerful rays kept it warmer than our side of the island. Dan and I walked under the fake palm tree shag entryway to the open-air restaurant. I sensed Catherine nearby.

"Table for two?" A woman in a blue shirt asked us.

I pointed toward a four-top on the far side of the patio area. A gorgeous couple sat with huge smiles on their faces and cocktails in their hands. The hostess nodded and we headed in that direction.

Most of the tables held people, and the bar to our right appeared full. There even appeared to be an inside area which, while undoubtedly nice, wasn't as appealing as remaining outside. The plentiful sunshine glimmered off the incredible expanse of turquoise water beyond the shorefront restaurant.

"Catherine? Alex?" I asked, and both stood. "Wow, you two are tall."

Catherine giggled and the drink she held aloft sloshed in her hand. "That we are." She embraced me and happiness washed over me. Life was so awesome. We were going to have such a good time.

I stepped back with a laugh. "Your energy is stronger than my protection barrier." As nice as her positive emotions felt, I surrounded them with a psychic bubble and released it, chanting under my breath that these were not my emotions.

"I'm Dan," my teammate introduced himself while I redirected the wayward energy.

"Welcome to Kona," Alex said. "Have a seat and let's get you some drinks."

Dan and I sat in the plastic slatted chairs at the round table, and the ocean beyond the gray stone wall pulled my gaze. I inhaled the salty air. "This is paradise."

"That's why we're here," Catherine said, and she and Alex clinked their glasses together. "I still can't believe we finally get to meet. In Hawaii, of all places."

"I know! We 'met'," I explained to Dan and Alex, using air quotes, "in a social media group for psychics, since we are variations on that theme. We both expected it to be filled with people who were either confused or liars," I said and lifted a single shoulder. "It stunned us to discover we might be who we said."

"On the internet, of all places." Catherine snort-laughed.

"How did you realize you were legit?" Dan asked.

"Catherine's talent agency exploits were covered extensively by the press," I explained. "I got curious."

"And, when Sarah called me, I knew she was telling the truth. That's what I do." She winked at Dan.

"We chat all the time about what's going on in our lives," I picked up the thread. "So, we know a lot about each other, but yep, this is our first in-person meeting." Although Dan still seemed a little lost, I moved on, figuring the details would come out over the course of happy hour. "We appreciate you taking the time during your honeymoon." I'd seen photos of her and her new husband online, plus our video chats, of course. Nothing prepared me for real life. Catherine's long blond hair flowed around a beautiful face, her blue eyes sparkling from paradise or alcohol, probably both. She wore a cute shades-of-purple multi-colored sundress that showed off the tiny bit of tan she was getting from the Hawaiian sun. Alex's longish dark hair framed a clean-cut chiseled face with electric green eyes. My hiking outfit was drab in comparison, though I reminded myself I was on a work trip. In any event, there was no question how the agent and actor came together. Although, I knew it wasn't smooth sailing at the beginning.

A waitress appeared, interrupting my musings. We placed orders for a couple of $5 Mai Tais. I also requested three tacos with a variety of meats and toppings. My growling stomach just wouldn't quit.

"You're a volunteer?" Alex asked Dan.

"I am. Not too bad a gig, when you get a free trip to Hawaii out of it," he joked.

My eyes rolled of their own accord, an action Catherine didn't miss. She waggled her eyebrows at me.

"How's the case going?" Alex continued, unaware of the faces Catherine and I were making at each other. Or ignoring us. Could be either, if I was honest.

I focused on the conversation and took the couple through our case. "So that's where we are," I concluded, swinging my hands with a big flourish and nearly taking out my drink. Talking with my hands meant this was not an uncommon occurrence for me. I must have missed the waitress bringing our drinks and tacos.

Catherine frowned. "I don't think I have anything constructive to add, to be honest. It sounds like the team has been very thorough and you're on the right track."

Alex sipped his glass. "I'd have to agree."

"No worries," I assured them both. "We appreciate hearing we're not missing anything major."

Catherine's eyes lasered in on mine. "How's it going, being in charge?"

I gulped my drink. "It's fine."

"You're lying," she said, though her lips twitched, fighting a smile.

"Not fair, talking to a human lie detector."

Dan startled beside me. "Wait, what? I thought you were an empath, similar to Sarah? Jeff really meant human lie detector when he said that at the hospital?"

"Like you're any better," Catherine said, plowing right past Dan's questions. "Miss I-Can-Literally-Feel-What-You're-Feeling."

I patted Dan's arm. "We should catch you up." I waved my hand at Catherine and Alex to do so, and dug into my tacos, enjoying the sound of the crunch and the taste of seasoning.

"Yes, I'm a human lie detector. Whenever someone speaks to me, an internal chime of sorts goes off to let me know if they've told the truth or if they've lied."

"No way," Dan mumbled.

Her brow furrowed. "It's not 100 percent, though. If someone has their own abilities, they can block me. Also, if they believe what they're saying, even if objectively it's not true, it'll ping as truth."

"And I'm a half-incubus," Alex explained, dropping his voice well below the din of the raucous happy hour crowd.

"Huh, that wasn't on my list of possibilities," Dan quipped. "What special skills do you have?"

"I can breathe in someone's essence and make them do or say whatever I want." Alex's deadpan face floored Dan.

"Totally feeling inferior at this table," Dan joked. "You can seriously do that?" At Alex's nod, Dan's eyes widened.

"But he almost never does," Catherine was quick to add, mock-frowning at her husband.

"Seems there would be ethics questions involved," Dan agreed.

"But that's an idea," she continued, snapping her fingers.

"It is? No, it's not," I disagreed.

She giggled again. "Not that. If you need me to help you with sussing out the truth, let me know."

"Maybe if we interview Helen a second time," I conceded. I didn't think she was lying. But if I could ask the right questions, Catherine's truth-or-lie ability could help me get a better handle on that unknown hostile energy. I'd keep that option in my back pocket.

"For now," I said, lifting my drink. The others did the same. "Let's celebrate the union of two beautiful people. And enjoy some more tacos."

CHAPTER SEVENTEEN

Hawaiʻi Volcanoes National Park stayed open 24 hours a day, but Dan and I had no intention of hiking in the dark. My alarm blared at 7 AM, and despite happy hour the previous evening, I jumped out of bed. Excitement mounted at the thought of hiking Kīlauea again. And, I'll admit, I was ready to do some more sneaking around.

I pulled on a hiking outfit that mirrored yesterday's, remembering the conversation with Jeff when he invited me on the trip. I'd asked how much clothing to bring, given that investigations could last a week, if not several weeks if a trail went cold for a time. He'd laughed and replied that the client wouldn't pay for weeks of a Hawaiian investigation. We tossed around the idea of 3-5 days, then settled on 7, to be safe. We couldn't imagine not having an answer by then; or that medical science wouldn't have one.

A knock on the door sounded while I was in the galley kitchen, pulling down cups and plates. The coffee pot burbled as it prepared to release the nectar of the gods. I crossed the terracotta floor to admit Dan, who was meeting me for breakfast before our hike.

Entirely too attractive for his own good, he smiled when he saw me. He also wore a replica of yesterday's hiking outfit, except the shirt was an earthy brown shade. Sunglasses perched on his head. I'd bring mine too, and hope the clouds would part to let the sun through for at least some of the day later.

"Come on in," I invited, heading back to the kitchen with Dan following.

"Can I help with anything?"

"Nah. I'm keeping it simple. Eggs and toast?"

"Perfect." He sniffed the air. "And I'll take some of that coffee if it's ready."

A glance confirmed it was, so I poured us both cups. We chatted about nothing while I cooked breakfast. Once we sat, he directed a small smile my way.

"You look good this morning."

"Uh-huh."

"Today could be a date."

"I'm ten years older than you."

"So you keep saying."

"And you're kind of an employee."

"When does the pay hit my bank account?"

We both laughed, knowing our little flirtation would never go anywhere. And not because of the issues I'd brought up. His personality was so earnest, he was like a puppy. I snorted and he looked inquisitively at me. "Let's plan our adventure," I said in response, and grabbed the park map I'd placed on the side of the table earlier.

I spread the map out between us, to review the best approach to the off-limits section of the volcano. "We'll basically do what I did last time. We'll drive on Crater Rim Drive as far as possible toward Kīlauea Overlook. Unless it changed, it should be the Steam Vents."

From there, we ate while we worked out our plan. A lot of it would depend on if there'd been any new fissures or cracks along the road, but I felt ready. We finished the last bites of our food before carrying the dishes to the sink.

"Let's head to the park," I said. We grabbed our backpacks with snacks and water, hopped in the SUV, and drove up the highway to the entrance, followed Crater Rim Drive again to the Steam Vents parking lot. We pulled in and snagged one of the few remaining open spots. Guess we weren't the only tourists up early.

"Ready to break the law," I said to Dan from the side of my mouth, in a lowered voice. Like the gangster that I was, clearly.

His eyes sparkled. "You know it."

We crossed Crater Rim Drive, keeping close to it, heading past the closed section. The key to going where you didn't belong was to act like you did. Nevertheless, as before, I flinched in anticipation of someone yelling at us to stop. Nobody did, so we kept going, soon reaching a sign for the Kīlauea Military Camp.

"Let's head inward toward the caldera," I suggested. "If I'm remembering the map and my previous steps correctly, the Crater Rim Trail is closest to Crater Rim Drive around here."

Dan nodded, concurring with my memory, saving me from having to dig the map out of my backpack and fumble with opening it. Cracks and sinkholes increased the further away from the road closure we got. We stepped over and around the desert scrub brush and groupings of trees. Quiet surrounded us, and the air smelled smoky.

I gasped.

"Are you okay?"

Hostility filled me. My stomach churned and my heart raced. The need to lash out overwhelmed me. It took a long moment to realize that wasn't my emotion. I concentrated on loosening my muscles and taking long, deep breaths. "We're getting close," I choked out.

"Strong emotion?"

No matter how I explained clairempathy to someone, something got lost in translation. It wasn't just sensing the emotions. I experienced the emotions themselves. And the stronger the emotions, the stronger the accompanying physical sensations. I glanced around, on the off chance other wayward tourists were breaking the rules too. Nobody was visible.

This was where I'd stopped last time, and now that I wasn't alone, nothing on earth was going to keep me from my goal. "Let's keep going," I said. We continued along Crater Rim Trail, the scent of ash rising with the temperature. This had to be from the lava incinerating plant life, according to my research. Low viscosity lava, like what was bubbling to the surface during this heightened eruption, rarely trapped gases, and thus would most likely not have an odor. Additional fissures appeared and soon we saw a faint glow of red in the distance. "Is that it?" My voice held a note of awe.

"We're almost there," Dan shouted and increased his pace.

Anger surged, bringing me to an abrupt halt. "Dan!" I cried out, then leaned over, hands on my knees, panting in agony. I heard quick footsteps before a hand on my back applied gentle pressure.

"It's okay," he murmured. "It's not your emotion."

"Shut up," I growled, and the pressure from his hand lifted.

"It's okay. It's not your emotion," he repeated, and the pressure returned.

So perceptive, my little puppy, I thought with a smile that became a grimace, as I fought with the foreign emotions. Years of experience with others' emotions and physical responses hadn't quite prepared me for the blunt force of this energy. I sat on the ground, barely withstanding the need to pound the earth, instead clutching handfuls of dirt. The tightness in my chest made it difficult to draw air, but apparently there was enough for me to growl my irritation at… something. Startled by the realization that I had nothing to be angry about, I slowly created my white bubble. The seething red hostility in my mind remained slippery, until eventually the bubble encased it. A lessening of the intensity followed and I rushed to fill it with reminders of my health and happiness. I was in Hawaii on a case and these emotions weren't mine. A true smile blossomed.

That positive thought and smile did the trick, and the energy withdrew. I inhaled and exhaled several deep breaths to calm my racing heart, before standing and striding forward, Dan scrambling to join me. We walked together, keeping the red glow in sight. Sweat trickled down the side of my face. A glance at Dan confirmed he was flushed and sweating too. No doubt in part due to the actual exertion, but also certainly due to the heat from the lava flow we were fast approaching.

We angled toward the direction from where the energy flowed. I gasped again, this time because of the lava dead ahead, not more than fifteen feet from us. Despite the lack of a gaseous smell, a wave of nausea hit me. I doubted the ash caused it, so I probed for an accompanying emotion, but there wasn't one. This might be purely physical.

"I don't feel so good," Dan said.

"We shouldn't get any closer."

"This is pretty cool, anyway."

"No doubt."

We stared at the bubbling lava, watching it glow bright then inch outward in all directions. He was right, this was by far the coolest thing I'd ever witnessed in person.

Undefined energy rolled over me, and I felt uncertain. "Pele?" I asked in response. Dan took a step from me and remained quiet while I explored the experience. "Are you here?" Amazingly, I didn't feel dumb at all asking a volcano goddess if she was present. Emotions flooded through me, almost on a loop. Hostility. Anger. Uncertainty. With each shifting emotion, a new physical sensation emerged. A headache started at the base of my skull. Nausea rose, threatening for me to vomit my breakfast from earlier. My skin crawled.

"What do you want?" I asked in desperation. No words came with the emotions, and I despaired that I would be unable to understand her message. If there was one. If it was Pele. The emotional whirlwind continued, driving me to my knees. Tears streamed down my face. Desire to scream tore a guttural sound from my throat.

"Sarah!" Dan called, worry etched in his yell.

I lifted a hand to keep him back, focusing on the energy swirling around and within me. I'd never felt such raw power before in my life. It could not be human. Was this a goddess's energy? My head dropped back and my eyes closed. I extended my arms to the sides, physically mirroring the opening up of my psyche. A bright light filled my mind. The anger climbed within and I cried out again, "What do you want?"

The hairs on my arms rose and I swore I heard a crackling noise. Lava? Manifested energy? I tried to form my white bubble around the incredible sensations. It popped. I tried again, starting with a marble-sized ball in my mind and slowly enlarging it. When it approached the bright light in my mind, it shattered. My eyes popped open and I stared straight ahead, waiting for the shards of my bubble to settle. They felt like tinkling in my brain, a not-altogether-unpleasant sensation. But the anger began to subside, and the desire to shout, yell, do something along with it. Understanding filled me – though of what I couldn't say – and I nodded.

"I'll do what I can," I promised, unaware that I'd reached that conclusion. With my uttering, the emotions vanished. I remained kneeling on the dirt, waiting for the headache and nausea to fade to tolerable levels. Then I stood and faced Dan, wiping the moisture from my cheeks.

"That was the most incredible thing I've ever felt."

"I'm not clairempathic, and I swear I felt something," he concurred.

I swayed on my feet, so we sat on the scrub-covered ground, observing the bubbling lava until I felt human again. After, of course, since at heart we were tourists, we snapped a billion photos of the lava, before returning the way we came.

Back at the SUV, Dan asked the question I'd been pondering. "What do you think that meant?"

My mouth opened and closed. How did I put into words what had happened? I couldn't. That level of power couldn't possibly be human. It couldn't possibly be solely Helen. Unless Helen possessed an insane level of previously latent power. She couldn't, could she? I shook my head and met Dan's eyes.

"I truly didn't believe I'd wind up saying this," I hedged. "But. In the absence of any other explanation, and in light of the power of what just happened, I'd say Helen somehow not only woke Pele, but riled her up. And we need to help her find peace before more people die."

CHAPTER EIGHTEEN

When Helen Richards agreed to meet with me, I anticipated returning to her home. Nope. I managed not to drop my jaw at the sight of her. Though my lack of a poker face betrayed me again.

"It's five o'clock somewhere," she said with a brittle smile, lifting a giant purple cocktail toward me in greeting. Not quite a fishbowl drink, it wasn't too far off. Taking her greeting as an invitation to sit, I pulled out the dark green chair and joined her.

Dan and I had headed back to the rental to get cleaned up. Then, I'd dropped him at the hospital to help our boss with his discharge. The doctor had deemed Jeff out of the woods and agreed to release him. So now I found myself with the woman who possibly started it all. At least she'd chosen an interesting, if surprising, locale for our meeting.

The Blue Hawaiian was a unique Big Island mainstay, a sort of hybrid of Rainforest Cafe and Hard Rock Cafe. From the moment you entered the restaurant, rhythm and blues played on the sound system. This provided the perfect backdrop to the rainforest motif, with deep green plastic plants hung alongside guitars and pictures of smiling celebrities on the walls. Not a large space, the high ceiling made it seem more spacious, and the tables allowed just enough room for your average tourist to squeeze past. Given the time, there weren't many tourists partaking, but I imagined the joint would jump during happy hour and dinner. If not for my intended purpose, I'd grab a cocktail and join her. Alas, I was there on business.

"What can I do for you?" Helen asked, her blue eyes veiled. She wore jeans and a stretchy brown top, her hair pulled off her face in a French braid. The flush to her cheeks left me wondering if this wasn't already her second or third cocktail. An uneaten burger and fries sat on a plate before her, the forlorn meal suggesting faked merriment.

"I'll get right to it," I assured her, before providing an abbreviated version of my visit to the park to see the lava. Helen's facial expressions left little chance of misunderstanding that she considered me an idiot.

"What does any of this have to do with me?" She took a huge drink of her oversized cocktail.

I hesitated. "This is going to sound crazy."

"Crazier than thinking Pele is real? And that you communicated with her?"

"Yes."

She set her drink down, gaze narrowing in on me.

"I think your hike to Kīlauea," I began, "somehow activated – for lack of a better word – the energy associated with Pele." This sounded better than 'you woke the goddess' but Helen's shrill laughter in response made me second-guess my word choice.

"Are you insane? You're insane," she answered herself. "I 'activated the energy associated with Pele'," she mimicked me, doing a remarkably impressive job. She took another large swig of her drink.

"I think you did," I responded, my voice quiet, yet firm.

"Let's say I believed you – which I don't – what do you want me to do about it?"

"Work with me to help Pele find peace."

Helen guffawed this time. "Seriously?"

"Seriously. I understand it sounds preposterous—"

"Completely bonkers, you mean."

"That too." I shook my head. "If you felt what I did out at the park…"

For the first time, she appeared uncertain, biting her lower lip.

"You did, didn't you?" I snapped my fingers. "You feel it still."

"I don't know what you're talking about," she insisted, punctuating her words with yet another large swallow of the purple cocktail.

"What's that you're drinking?" I asked, attempting to calm the conversation for a moment. It worked.

"It's 'Pele's Revenge'." My eyes widened and she chortled. "I made that up. You should see your face."

My cheeks heated. "Well played."

"Thank you." Helen placed the drink on the table and leaned toward me, elbows splayed. "Listen. I can appreciate you have a job to do. But you're barking up the wrong tree." Her voice rose. "People are dying? I. Don't. Care. They shouldn't be cheaters."

I nodded, anger rising within me. She was right. Righteousness filled me.

"Promising to love someone and stay faithful, those aren't just words," she continued, blue eyes bright with her rage.

"No, they aren't," I said, wanting to shout in agreement.

"Fool me once, shame on you. Fool me twice, shame on me," she said, then took a swig and looked away.

Her words startled me in their unexpectedness. And they could only mean one thing. "He cheated on you before."

Heat suffused her face. "You never stop, do you?"

I gave her a lopsided grin and pretended that was a compliment. "No, I don't."

She glared at me for a long moment. "Fine. We were only married for five years. He cheated on me two years ago. That was the first time. He swore it was a mistake, that he still loved me, and I forgave him. I took him back. Fool me once," she whispered this last into her cocktail before gulping the purple elixir.

"I'm sorry," I said, knowing the words were inadequate.

Sure enough, she waved away my empty words. "As I said the first time we met," she continued, "cheaters deserve whatever fate – or Pele – decides to mete out. Period."

I barely withstood the urge to yell my agreement. Helen broke eye contact and I struggled to regain my own emotions.

"Whatever," she said into her glass. "I want to enjoy my cocktails."

Ragged breaths sounded in my ears and I realized that was me. I filled my lungs and held the breath, reminding myself that I wasn't angry. These powerful emotions were Helen's, not mine. A shadow of doubt formed in the back of my mind. The energy felt so similar to what I'd experienced on the hike. Was that because Helen was channeling Pele, or was all of this only Helen? Could I have still been feeling her at the park, even without physical proximity? It didn't seem likely. But. I reconsidered the idea that she'd had latent supernatural abilities awoken by her strong negative emotions. Right now, though, the question was academic. It was more important that I reach her and bring her to our side. I fortified my stone wall of protection and released her anger.

"Helen—"

She cut me off, her tone brooking no argument. "Just stop." She sighed. "I'm done with this. I've told you I don't care. Alan deserved what he got. Your client, or client's brother, whatever, deserves it. If they can't keep it in their pants, they deserve whatever comes their way." Her glittering eyes captured mine. "I'm also telling you one time, and one time only. Stop trying to help them."

"What do you mean?"

"You know what I mean. Just stop."

"You know I can't do that. I won't."

"Then, I can't be responsible for what happens next." She returned her gaze to the purple drink and waved her hand, dismissing me.

I rose shakily to my feet and without a word headed for the exit. The cloudy sky when I stepped out of the building matched my mood. At least the conversation wasn't a complete bust. The energy surrounding Helen almost matched the energy I'd felt hiking Kīlauea. A connection existed. I was no longer as certain Pele caused the fever-illness; and that was a bit of a relief, to be honest. But a scorned woman with uncontrolled supernatural abilities was dangerous too. The possible meaning behind her final statement reverberated in my head as I drove to join Dan and Jeff at the hospital.

Was she threatening me?

CHAPTER NINETEEN

My phone sounded an incoming text from Mandie as I entered the hospital, before I thought to silence the ringer.

Lacie Roberts died.

Oh no.

That made the third death from the fever-illness. I'd never made it back to speak with her after she'd been admitted to the hospital. The memory of her sweaty, short blond hair, tired brown eyes, and no makeup on a flushed face leapt to mind. I hoped her passing was peaceful, but knew I couldn't dwell on the death. Since the Christians couldn't remember when Natalie hiked the volcano, I wasn't sure if Lacie died earlier than Alan's timeline or not. And, thus, what her death meant for the others who were sick. I hurried to Jeff's room, not surprised that he was still there with Dan awaiting discharge.

"This looks like progress," I said upon entering and seeing Jeff sitting, in jeans and a University of Miami sweatshirt, next to the bed and not in it. The lack of beeping monitors reassured me.

He chuckled. "It's a minor miracle we got this far. The nurse stuck her head in about thirty minutes ago to say the discharge paperwork was almost complete and that I could change."

"I assume Mandie texted you both," I said, not asked.

They nodded; expressions solemn. "That makes three," Dan stated.

"Do we know how Cameron, Patricia, and Kevin are doing?" I asked.

"Last I checked," Dan answered, "they all have fevers over 104, and the other symptoms vary. Cameron is still holding his own, but the cooling methods are becoming less effective."

"Were they ever effective?" This wasn't Jeff knocking the hospital protocol, just recognizing what seemed to be a pretty obvious pattern.

The sides of my mouth pulled down and I gave a small shake of my head before answering for Dan. "Not really. This all seems to be a function of time more than anything else."

"Did you run here?" Jeff asked, squinting at me.

"No, why?" His non sequitur confused me.

"You seem a little flushed."

I touched my face. Was it warm? I didn't think so. "Maybe I hustled more than I thought," I said with uncertainty. My phone vibrated an incoming notification in concert with Dan and Jeff's phones ringing. Guess I was the only one to put my phone on silent. We all checked and then I answered Mandie's video chat for the group.

"Hey Mandie, what's going on?" I greeted our researcher. We could hear a broadcast airing in the background.

"Have you guys seen the news?" She asked instead of answering.

The three of us said no and she turned her phone to face her computer screen, where a live report was happening. The corner writing identified it as KITV in Hilo. A pretty dark-haired woman, maybe native Hawaiian, sat behind a desk in a studio, appearing suitably grim.

"—unexplained deaths," she finished a sentence. "There are three additional known victims of this unidentified illness, but there may be many more unknown. If you have developed symptoms consistent with hyperthermia, including fever, nausea, chills, dizziness, or headache, please reach out to your doctor. Or, if you feel your life is in danger, go to your local emergency department."

Mandie muted the broadcast and swung her phone back around. She'd pulled her curly brown hair off her face in a messy bun. "The good news is that if there are additional sick people, this should bring them out. The bad news is that the medical establishment is about to be swamped with people who think they're dying."

"Yeah." I agreed with Mandie's bad news assessment more than the good. "There's going to be mass hysteria, and that might mask any actual victims." I glanced from Jeff to Dan and back to Mandie. "Keep your trawler searching, but we'll put it on the back burner for now." I looked at the men. "Our focus – well, Jeff, we're dropping you off at the house." I held up a hand to stop his objections.

"No argument. Mandie, Dan, and I will focus on identifying a new plan of attack. We have some evidence to suggest a supernatural force is at the root cause of this fever-illness. We don't know if it's all Helen Richards, if she's channeling Pele, or if Pele is acting independently." I counted days off on my fingers. "Tomorrow's Day Eight for Cameron. If his illness course matches our first victim's, he has two days. If we're lucky, it won't be that precise. We need ideas for resolving the negative emotions fueling the force, whether it's Helen, Pele, or some combination of them."

"Let's grab dinner on our way back to the rental and get some rest tonight," Jeff said. "That way we can all—" Here he stopped and directed a pointed look at me. "—spend the morning researching and brainstorming ideas to address those three scenarios just outlined."

I took a long pull from my water bottle before responding. "Resting tonight to let our subconscious minds percolate and then research in the morning sounds good." Now I returned Jeff's pointed look. "I imagine the next days are going to be rather hectic and we'll need to be ready to go at a moment's notice. We can discuss at that time who will do what."

Jeff smirked though lowered his head briefly in a show of understanding of my concern for his physical wellbeing, and, more importantly, his agreement. He wasn't going to end up back in the hospital due to stress from the case.

A nurse chose that moment to enter the room, cheerfully announcing that the paperwork was finished and Jeff could be discharged. She assisted him into a wheelchair; he recognized the hospital policy, so didn't even try a weak effort to resist. Dan started to follow the two as she wheeled our boss out the door, and I placed my hand on his arm to stop him.

"I wasn't kidding about the next days being hectic," I said. "We're coming down to the wire for our remaining known victims. I'd like to not have to tell Andrea Helms that her brother died. But I'd really like to not have to tell Chrissie that her husband refused to follow medical advice and had a second heart attack."

Dan's eyes widened. He'd met Chrissie McCarthy at a welcome-to-the-team barbeque we'd used as an excuse for a party. She was a petite firecracker, to put it mildly. It would not go well if something avoidable happened to Jeff. Since Dan would be staying with Jeff in the rental, the lion's share of the responsibility would fall on him to monitor Jeff.

"Understood," he said. "I foresee researching from the apartment in the morning and napping in the afternoon for Jeff."

"Fingers crossed," I replied before we hurried to follow Jeff and the nurse to the elevator. We'd just gotten Jeff out of the hospital. There was no reason for him to risk going back in. He could consult via phone, like Mandie.

It would be all we needed for a member of the team to go down and be out of commission at the climax of the case.

CHAPTER TWENTY

The bedroom fireplace must put off quite a lot of heat. I flung the sheets off of me and stretched, uncomfortably aware of being drenched in sweat. I squinted at the fireplace, which was off. Hmm. Of course, I turned it off when I went to bed; no reason to risk asphyxiation in the middle of the night if the gas fireplace malfunctioned.

So the sixth day of my island adventure dawned with my having a probable fever. I slowly took stock of the rest of my body, starting with my toes, moving up my legs, through my digestive tract, and then ending with my upper extremities and head. No aches or nausea. That was good. Maybe I didn't have a fever. Maybe I simply overheated during the night. It wasn't outside the realm of possibility.

I swung my legs over the side of the bed and sat up. No dizziness or vertigo. My stomach chose that moment to growl. Hunger, another good sign. I stood up, stretching my arms overhead and making fists with my toes, my socks bunching up against the hard floor. The morning would be low-key, conducting research and video chatting with Mandie as we found items of interest. I'd take it easy. In the meantime, I still felt warm, so I dressed in loose gray hiking shorts and a black tank top. I pulled my hair up into an attempt at a bun, most of the hair more or less captured by the hairband I grabbed off the bathroom counter.

In the kitchen, I set the coffee to brew and grabbed a yogurt. A quick group text alerted Jeff, Dan, and Mandie that I was up and moving about. Mandie, of course, would have risen hours ago, and was possibly eating a late lunch while I had my breakfast. The coffee's aroma got my synapses firing and I poured myself a cup to go with my food.

I grabbed my laptop and created a workspace for myself at the small oak table in the sitting area. The lush greenery outside made me glad for the window opposite. A quick review of email while I enjoyed breakfast, and I was ready to dive into the research. Where to start?

A brief history of Pele was in order. I'd already known of her from my mythology background, and we'd confirmed she was the goddess of fire and volcanoes, and also specifically of passion and jealousy. But what was her story? I typed in *Pele Goddess of Fire* and started reading.

Most sites agreed on the basics. Pele traveled the Earth, looking for a home for her fire, and did not find success until she reached Hawaii. Now, the Big Island was sort of her area of influence, with her home becoming Halemaʻumaʻu at the summit caldera of Kīlauea. She battled with her sister Nāmaka, and although Pele died in that battle, her spirit lived on in the volcano. Now she controlled the power of creation, in large part through her lava flows. She also threw bolts of lava when angry and had a violent temper. That didn't sound good. I supposed I should be grateful, if indeed Pele had awoken and was responsible for the current illness, that at least she wasn't throwing bolts of lava at people.

That was sort of the CliffsNotes version. There were many additional stories of her interactions within her family and with humanity. What I found more interesting, however, were stories of Pele sightings. They went back hundreds of years: people reporting powerful feelings at the volcano or claiming to have captured photos of her in the lava. Others even claimed she approached them as a beautiful young woman or frail old woman, asking for help. And woe was you if you didn't offer to help her. Those didn't quite fit with our current supernatural conundrum, but they supported the notion that a supernatural influence was possible.

I glanced at the clock on the laptop, noted it was too early for lunch. Some kettle chips sounded perfect to snack on, so that's what I grabbed. In between bites of the deliciousness, I sent more texts to the team. Mandie said she'd be ready to chat in about an hour. Dan confirmed Jeff was napping, so I invited him over for the video chat later. A bead of sweat rolled down my face and I grimaced.

Unless I removed all my clothes, I couldn't wear less. There weren't many windows in the rental, but I made my way around to open all three, enjoying the rush of cool air that flowed over my apparently feverish skin.

Even though I doubted the effectiveness, I swallowed some acetaminophen and popped my cooling neck wrap in the freezer. Better than nothing. Two big questions loomed in my mind. And I knew just the person to run them by.

"Hey Mom."

"Peanut, it's good to hear from you," my mother's warm voice came through the line. And, yeah, that's her nickname for me. I got the only short gene in the family somehow. "I thought you were in Hawaii this week."

"I am."

"How can I help?"

I smiled at the question. Dr. Stephanie Danger was a clairempath too, though her affinity was for animals; and that made her Houston's most sought-after veterinarian. No, her question came from pure mother instinct. "Let me catch you up."

"That's quite the conundrum," she concluded when I finished.

"And it leads to two big questions," I said, bringing me back to what I'd thought of prior to calling. "Is this all in my head? Or am I now on my own countdown to further illness?"

"Those aren't the questions you have, I don't think."

"No?" I sat back down at the table to wait for her explanation.

"I think it's bigger than that."

My chin dropped. "Am I dying?"

"And what do you think?" She'd honed her compassionate clinical tone through years of veterinary practice.

"I might be," I conceded before defiantly raising my chin. "But you know me, I'm also fairly confident I'll survive. Um, just in case, though…"

"You wanted to call your mom." I could hear the smile in her voice.

"Yeah." I coughed. "I love you, Mom. Tell Dad and my sibs I love them, too."

"I love you, too, Peanut. And, I will. But, it's going to be okay."

We disconnected the call and feeling buoyed by the conversation, I pondered the possibilities of my original questions, plus the bigger question of my threatened mortality. Was it all in my head? Was I now on a countdown to further illness? Or was I truly dying? Assuming the first and not the final (pun intended), I wondered when it began, because that could have bearing on whether Pele or Helen was the source.

It could have started with either of my hikes to the mountain, like the others. The first was thwarted, but I'd felt such raw power the second time. Except Dan hadn't reported being ill, and I wasn't involved in an illicit love affair. It just didn't seem likely. That left my solo encounter with Helen during her happy hour, providing more evidence that Helen was the source. Not that it changed our team's approach. We still didn't know if Helen's own active supernatural ability caused the illness, or if a more latent ability allowed her to channel Pele's power.

A knock on the door startled me. Had it been an hour already? I rose from the chair and headed across the rental to admit Dan, stopping in the kitchen to grab my now cooled neck wrap from the freezer. I pulled it over my head before opening the door.

"Hey doc," Dan greeted me, looking again like he stepped off the pages of a hiking magazine.

"Not yet," I replied with a small shake of my head.

He quirked an eyebrow and stared at the neck gaiter.

"I'm a little warm," I responded with a one-shoulder shrug. He followed me into the kitchen. "Grab yourself some coffee."

"The windows are open," he continued while he poured himself a cup.

"Thought some fresh air would be nice."

Now his eyes took in my relatively skimpy outfit, given the sixties temperature outside. "Anything you want to tell me?"

A quick consideration of the truth. "Just a restless night's sleep," I sidestepped. Why worry him, when there was nothing he could do?

CHAPTER TWENTY-ONE

"Hey Mandie." We exchanged pleasantries via video chat and then got down to business. I caught her and Dan up on what I'd already read.

"That's consistent with what I found," Mandie agreed, "and like we said yesterday, it's one of three options. All Helen Richards; Helen, but she's channeling Pele; or Pele acting alone. So far, today's research doesn't eliminate any of those possibilities."

I must have made a noise because Dan gave me an inquisitive look. "Did you learn something else?" Mandie leaned closer to her phone, as if she could see me better to understand what he was responding to.

"Um," was my immediate reply while my brain scrambled to decide what to do.

"What aren't you telling us, doc?" Dan asked.

"Not yet," I said by rote before sighing. "I think I can eliminate the possibility of it being Pele acting alone."

Mandie's eyebrows shot skyward. "You can? How?"

"Yeah, how, Sarah?" Dan asked. I didn't miss the deliberate use of my name.

My cheeks heated, and I wondered idly if the red tint was visible through my already flushed skin. "I'm pretty sure I'm infected, affected, whatever."

"What?" Mandie's voice screeched through the phone.

"I knew it," Dan mumbled.

"Why didn't you say something?" Mandie asked.

"I didn't want to worry anybody, so I was going to wait it out until we solved the case." I grinned, but they both stared at me in stony silence. "Okay, okay. Remember yesterday how Jeff asked if I had run to his room because I was flushed? This morning I woke up hot, and unable to cool off." I pointed to my shorts and tank top. "Thus, the outfit, the cooling thing, and the open windows." This last I directed more to Dan, who gave his head a small shake.

"We're a team. You don't keep things from the team," Mandie chastised me.

"I won't do it again," I promised.

"Wait. So how does that eliminate one of our possibilities?"

I hid a smile at her back-to-business question; I knew she wouldn't stay mad at me. Now I was excited to share what I'd surmised. "Dan and I hiked the volcano where there have been sightings of Pele in the lava, and where the wives of our victims have hiked prior to their husbands and lovers getting sick," I recapped. "However, neither of us got sick following our hike."

"I guess that's because we're not lovers," Dan said, waggling his eyebrows.

"Behave, youngster," I admonished. "Anyway, I didn't start to feel warm until after I met with Helen and she told me to stop interfering."

"She threatened you?" Mandie asked.

"Not in so many words. The comment, as I recall, was, 'I can't be responsible for what happens next.' Not a direct threat, but a veiled one."

"Okay, I agree," Mandie said. "Based on the timing and interactions, we can surmise it's not Pele operating on her own as our agent of infection." She waved her hand. "Or whatever. That leaves Pele channeled by Helen or Helen's abilities acting on her knowledge of Pele, with or without her direct intent. If there's a supernatural element," she added, to be thorough, I imagined. Dan nodded his agreement. "I'm thinking our next step is to research any instances of humans channeling what is believed to be Pele's energy."

"Makes sense. We'll still want to come up with a possible intervention if it's Helen alone. Since it undoubtedly will be more complicated if Helen is channeling Pele, we ought to see if someone has done that before. Or believed to have done that," I qualified my words. I presumed, at this point, that there was a supernatural element, but you could never be certain about these things.

"Why don't we take an hour to run some more internet searches and then compare notes?" Mandie suggested.

"Sounds good," I agreed and Dan echoed. We said our goodbyes and disconnected the chat. "Not a word."

He held up his hands in mock surrender. "I wasn't going to say anything." He leaned back in the chair and crossed his arms over his chest.

"Of course, you were."

He smirked. "Yeah, I was. And I am. Why would you not tell me about the fever? I directly asked you what was going on." The hurt in his voice made me wince.

"There's nothing you or the team can do," I reasoned. "Why have you worry about something you can't control?"

He opened his mouth to speak, then closed it. "We're a team," he finally said, though I sensed he planned to say something else.

When he didn't continue, I barreled on. "Ready to research?" I offered a broad smile, and although he may have wanted to object to my topic and tone changes, he didn't.

"You know it."

We both rose from the table to refresh our coffees. After that, we remained quiet except for the sound of typing while we searched the internet for instances of humans channeling Pele. I didn't know about Mandie or Dan, but my initial searches were not fruitful. Mainly I found examples of channeling Pele's energy as part of a spiritual practice, such as 'channeling your inner goddess'.

Though it was kind of cool to see women using the strengths of Pele to strengthen themselves. Cool, but not useful. I rested my chin on my hand, elbow on the table, wracking my brain for better search terms.

About an hour later, it was time to share what we'd learned. Mandie went first. "I couldn't find any current examples of humans channeling a god's or goddess's powers like this. But I found ancient references to Pele as a 'goddess who talked', known as akua noho, and she could possess a human, who would become Pele's kahu." She frowned. "It doesn't quite fit our scenario, however, since Helen doesn't appear to be possessed. Though it suggests precedent for powers flowing through a human."

Dan and I nodded, then he presented his results. "I only found mediums as examples of humans channeling powers, so not the same. But I found ideas to placate an angry goddess, and Pele specifically. Two are to make an offering, or ho'okupu, and a prayer, or pule." He chuckled. "Offering her gin was mentioned a lot. There were examples since the 1700s, from after gin was introduced to the island, that when in human form, Pele prefers gin."

"I wonder if Helen's happy hour drink contained gin. If so, that theory is a bust," I said. We burst into laughter.

"That's all I have," he concluded. They looked at me.

"I'll piggyback on you both. I also, sadly, didn't find any current examples of humans channeling Pele's powers like we're theorizing. But I found examples of prayers and ceremonies related to Pele's curse that may be relevant."

"Pele's curse?" Dan asked.

133

"Turns out tourists take rocks, sand, sticks, and such for souvenirs. In 1946, a park ranger got tired of people stealing these things, despite it being illegal. So, he created the notion of the curse. Experts disagree on whether there's a reference to anything like this in Hawaii's cultural mythology. Some say there's no connection, and it's frankly offensive. Others suggest that's not true. They say that since rocks have personalities – even genders! – removing them from Pele and the volcano is a bad idea. Whether it truly brings bad luck is anybody's guess. Experts recommend performing a ceremony to apologize, seek forgiveness, and release the energy back to Pele."

"I like that," Mandie interjected. "Maybe we modify a ceremony to seek forgiveness and release Pele's anger back to her?"

"How do we do that? And will it work if it's just Helen's own super-active abilities?" Dan mused.

I carried the phone to an open window and stood before it. Dan followed, brow furrowed and lips tightened with worry. The cool breeze felt better, even if I doubted it was doing much beyond the surface.

A trio of dings announced notifications of a text to all three of us. That could only be Jeff. I kept my phone on the video chat, while Dan checked the incoming message.

"Jeff's up and hungry," he said.

"Mandie," I directed to the screen. "We'll talk with you later." She nodded and I disconnected the chat.

Dan texted Jeff. "I've told him to meet us outside and we'll catch him up over lunch."

CHAPTER TWENTY-TWO

"Are you sure you're up for this?" I asked Jeff when Dan and I joined him at our SUV. He looked okay for having been discharged yesterday from the hospital. *But they discharged him yesterday from the hospital.* So there was that.

"I'm fine to go sit and eat," he retorted. He peered closer at me, in my shorts and tank top in the overcast sixty-degree weather, with my auburn hair pulled back.

I broke eye contact and headed toward the driver-side door.

"Are you okay?" Jeff asked over the sound of doors opening and closing.

"Just a little warm," I semi-answered.

Dan made a pfft noise and, since he was in the seat behind mine, I glared at him in the rearview mirror. He gave a wry smile.

"What's going on?" Jeff asked, glancing between me and Dan.

I sighed. "There's a chance I may have the fever-illness."

"What?" The alarm deepened Jeff's voice and his spike of anxiety jumped my heart rate.

"Oh, yeah, I haven't updated you on my second meeting with Helen."

"And?"

"She told me she couldn't be held responsible for what happened next when I declined to stop investigating. I think this is what happened next." I shrugged under my seatbelt, feigning nonchalance. Jeff just had a heart attack; it couldn't be good for his heart for his adrenaline to spike.

Jeff shifted in his seat to stare at me. "Do you need to go to the hospital?" His question suggested he would accept only an affirmative answer. Which was not going to happen.

"It's okay," I tried to reassure him. "Some increasing heat. It's only the second day, and I have no other symptoms yet. Our best option is to solve this case," I reasoned, though I swore a bead of sweat formed on my forehead. Was that his anxiety, my anxiety, or the fever-illness? I needed to stop this unhelpful line of thought.

Thankfully, we reached the same cute little restaurant we'd eaten at before. I swung into the parking lot and we traipsed inside. The high ceilings with wooden beams drew my eye again. At the waitress's gesture to sit anywhere, we headed toward a four-top near the back wall.

I watched Dan survey the interior as I had on my first visit.

"You must like the fake candles," he said, knowing my ridiculous allergy situation.

I took a deep, unencumbered breath. "Very much so."

Marie, our waitress from last time, approached the table, her brown hair in a similar messy bun, black apron over her white shirt and black pants. "Aloha. Welcome back," she greeted us with a wide smile. "What can I bring you?"

I looked at the men. "Waters all around?" They nodded. "We'll need a minute with the menus."

"Of course." She left to get the water and we perused the menus. After she returned and we ordered some sandwiches, we got down to business.

"Given the timing of my illness, we've ruled out Pele operating independently of Helen," I began my summary, then sucked down half my glass of water, ignoring the concerned expressions on Jeff's and Dan's faces. I couldn't shake how parched I felt.

After bringing Jeff up to speed, I offered our conclusion. "Ultimately our goal is to calm down Pele. And we probably need to go through Helen."

"What is your idea for Helen?" Jeff asked. "All of those seem odd with an angry human," he added with a shrug.

"Given the popularity of gin in island drinks, we made a bit of an assumption that gin didn't work as an offering," I said, and explained to Jeff what we'd found about Pele maybe preferring gin in her human form. "But, honestly,

I'm not sure. Gin could still be an appropriate offering. That one just maybe feels like something the gin industry created to boost sales." The men chuckled. "In any event, people pray for others all the time. We also do ceremonies for rites of passage. People routinely ask deities for forgiveness. I would think versions of any of these could work."

"That makes sense," Jeff conceded. "You're probably on the right track, regardless of the approach. If the goal is to calm down Helen so that can solve the issue, calm down Pele herself, or break a channel to Pele if one exists, what's the best way to calm Helen?"

"I already tried appealing to her, but Helen's anger and hurt are strong," I answered. Marie arrived with our food and we ate our sandwiches in silence, pondering other possibilities. The pineapple vinaigrette on my veggie sandwich distracted me before my mind returned to swirling with those possibilities. We finished our sandwiches with nary a suggested thought.

"Anybody?" I asked. The men shook their heads. Marie appeared with the check, which Jeff paid.

"Mahalo," Marie said cheerfully, returning Jeff's credit card to him.

"Mahalo," we echoed.

When I paused in pushing back my chair to stand, the gentlemen followed suit. I snapped my fingers. "I have an idea."

"Great, let's hear it," Jeff said.

"My appealing to Helen didn't work, likely because I have no skin in the game," I said, slowly, piecing together my fragmented thoughts. "Why should she care what I think? I'm not a scorned wife, right?"

The men nodded, despite the confusion that showed on their faces.

"What about if someone who is directly affected spoke to her?" I suggested.

"One of the other wives?" Dan asked.

"Yes." I nodded like a bobble-head.

"That's an intriguing idea," Jeff said. "Natalie Christian or Paula Helms?"

I thought for a moment. "I'd say Natalie."

"How come?" Dan asked. "Paula is the wife of our client's brother. She may have more of an incentive to help."

"True. But, as mercenary as this might sound, Lacie Roberts died."

"I don't understand," Dan asked around a bite of meatball hoagie.

"Natalie told me she thought she and Kevin could repair their marriage—"

Dan jumped in. "With Lacie out of the picture, so to speak, Natalie may see that as better for her fixing her relationship."

"Exactly. She was in a pretty good headspace about the whole affair, to be honest. She might be open to this plan," I concluded.

"It's risky." Jeff shook his head.

I paused with my straw at my lips. "How do you mean?"

Jeff set his sandwich down and leaned in his chair, warming to the idea. "If she's already okay with the possibility of his leaving her, she may not be able to convey how important it is for her to get her husband back."

"Hmm. I hadn't considered that." I closed my eyes for a moment, gripping the table with both hands when I experienced vertigo. That wasn't good. I opened my eyes and released the table. Jeff was frowning at me and Dan's eyes had narrowed. Guess they hadn't missed any of that. I was glad they chose not to comment, though. "Natalie needs to express how much she loves her husband and how much their kids need their father," I continued.

"Wouldn't Helen already know that? She doesn't seem to be a dumb woman," Dan said.

"Let's ask Mandie." I didn't appreciate that the men were against my plan. She answered on the first ring, and I put her on speakerphone before presenting my suggestion. "What do you think?"

"Ooh, I'm not sure. What other options are there?"

"Is it possible she might be too okay with her marriage ending?" Jeff chimed in.

"That's a possibility," Mandie agreed. "I'd be more concerned about two cheated-on wives commiserating. Natalie said all the right things to you, Sarah. But who knows if that's how she really feels?"

I thought back to my brief interview with Natalie Christian in the hospital waiting room. "Now I don't know," I admitted. "I didn't fully lower my protective shields, given the ridiculously heightened emotions present. Her emotions didn't contain any anger and her grief felt real. I took that to mean she was honest about her emotional level. Though it's never 100 percent."

"That's a lot of ifs," Jeff said. "I have a bad feeling."

I dug my heels in. "Are we ready to jump to the goddess placating prayers and ceremonies? Or does anybody have another idea?"

Nobody did, so I called Natalie Christian and laid out my plan. She jumped at the chance to speak with Helen Richards.

This would work. I knew it. Well, I hoped. No, I knew it. Gah, was I trying to convince myself, or did I truly believe it?

This would work, I repeated to myself. Yes.

CHAPTER TWENTY-THREE

It didn't work. In fact, it failed spectacularly. But, let me back up.

Natalie beat me to Helen's home. I didn't know if she lived closer, or drove a lot faster than me, but there she was. She sat in a white four-door sedan, messing with her cellphone, her blond hair pulled into a low ponytail. I parked beside her in the SUV. Sensing my movement upon exiting, she stopped her activity on the phone and joined me. We stood awkwardly in the driveway before I broke the silence.

"Thank you for meeting me and agreeing to help," I said. Jeff and Dan had reluctantly agreed to remain at the rental house, in the interests of not overwhelming Helen. And, to be honest, not having a male presence at all. I'd dropped them there before driving here.

Natalie offered a crooked smile. "Of course." Her tired eyes and deeper worry lines on her face shocked me. Or maybe I was projecting my own worry. I confirmed my protection barrier had all its stones in place before heading to the house.

She followed me up the stairs, under the patio gazebo, and to the front door of Helen's sky-blue two-story home. I lifted my hand to knock, but the door opened before I made contact. I wasn't sure if the fact that she was watching us was a good thing or not. It's not like I'd called ahead. Perhaps I should have called ahead. Although, in retrospect, I doubt it would have made a difference.

"Good afternoon, Helen, apologies for the intrusion," I began. "This is Natalie Christian. She's in … was in … the same boat as you," I trailed off, realizing I ought to have rehearsed what I planned to say. "Helen, if you have some time, we'd like to come in and speak with you," I requested in a more assured voice.

Helen cocked her head at us before moving aside to allow entry. Natalie and I entered, and without additional guidance, headed past the bright foyer to the living room. A citrus scent tickled my nose, and I remembered it from my first visit. I still couldn't tell if it was a cleaning product, an extinguished candle, or something else. Not that it mattered. I stifled a sneeze. The painting that had caught my eye before drew my gaze again, and I confirmed it almost certainly depicted Pele in her volcanic glory. Natalie and I sat on the covered couch, with Helen sitting on the white wicker chair, as before.

"Thank you for seeing us," I said. Helen inclined her head in acknowledgment. "As I said, Natalie found herself in the same predicament, and I wanted to give her the opportunity to speak with you." Time for full honesty. "I'm hoping to persuade you to help us stop the deaths."

A small smile played on Helen's lips and a rush of annoyance flooded. I mirrored her smile before realizing the emotion wasn't mine. How did her irritation overtake my barrier so easily? I fortified my barrier again, though with less confidence.

"I doubt you'll be able to do so. You're welcome to try." Helen waved her hand at Natalie.

"Tell her what we talked about," I encouraged Natalie.

She smoothed nonexistent wrinkles from her gray slacks, silver bracelets tinkling. "I wanted to thank you."

Wait, what?

Natalie reached for Helen's hands across the small coffee table. When their fingers intertwined, confusion shot through me.

Did Natalie already know Helen?

Natalie continued. "I wasn't sure what I wanted for an outcome, but when the cheating scumbag became ill, I had a moment of clarity."

"This isn't what you told me—" I tried to interject and she steamrolled over me.

"When his bimbo girlfriend died, I cheered."

I swallowed audibly, and then elation filled me. Everyone was getting what they should. Cheaters deserved what they got.

"Now I'm just waiting for him to die," Natalie continued.

Exactly. They should all die— whoa, hold up. That definitely wasn't me. Still, it surged. I struggled to control the hostility. Often, the mere recognition of an other-emotion was enough to squash it. But the women's negativity had amplified and swamped my defenses. I searched within myself for the happiness over the deaths and illnesses, wrapped it in a bubble, and then released it. My horror at the turn of the conversation returned.

"What about your kids? Don't they deserve a father," I tried frantically.

Natalie turned flashing eyes on me. "They deserve a role model who can keep it in his pants."

Helen laughed.

This wasn't going well. At. All.

"I don't know how you did it," Natalie addressed Helen, expression triumphant. "But you're alright with me. If he dies, great. If he doesn't, I'll be divorcing him once he's discharged from the hospital."

"I honestly don't know if or how I'm doing it," Helen unexpectedly confided. "If I am, you're welcome. And I won't change a thing. I agree with you." The women exchanged conspiratorial looks.

I blanched. "Helen, you can't be serious."

"Oh, I am. I have no problem if all cheaters die. This will be what's best for everyone. Like Natalie said, children deserve good role models. Cheaters aren't good role models." She shrugged.

I started to reply and then realized Helen's emotions were rising in me again. Except there was a difference. When I isolated the emotions to release them, I sensed something beneath the anger that I couldn't identify. Ambivalence? Was that even an emotion? I tried to reach inward and it burrowed further away.

Helen released Natalie's hands and rose. "You can go now," Helen said to me, though Natalie also stood when I did a beat after. Nobody spoke while we walked to the front door, then Helen opened it and ushered us out.

"Please think about what's happening," I urged her before she could close the door. My stomach clenched hard and a sense of disquiet rocked me back. The door slammed in my face, but I was too focused on what I'd felt. That had to be the ambivalence from earlier. Some part of Helen didn't agree with what was going on.

"Too-da-loo," Natalie said in a sing-song voice before blowing me a kiss and – I swear on my life – prancing down the stairs.

"Wait," I called out, hurrying down after her.

She faced me, hand on cocked hip. "What?"

"What happened in there?" I asked when I reached her. We stood at the front of her car.

"You heard everything," she said, then she frowned.

"What? What is it?"

"I, um, nothing," she said, abruptly moving away from me.

I reached for her arm to stop her. "I don't understand." I imagined my protective wall a little lower, to try to get more information. Anger and resistance surged within me, stronger than I would have thought. While I probed, the emotions decreased and bewilderment replaced them.

Her tear-filled eyes met mine. "I'm not sure what happened. I mean," her voice dropped to a barely audible volume, "part of me wanted him to be punished. But what I said in there…" She shook her head. "I don't know. Everything happens for a reason, I guess." Before I could respond, she darted around to enter her car. The vehicle backed up a moment later, and the tires squealed when she gunned the engine.

Natalie seemed genuinely perplexed. Why? She admitted to wanting Kevin punished. Surely Helen (or Pele!) couldn't have amplified that negativity. Nausea rose within me and I wondered at the source. Residual emotion from the women? An increase in the fever-illness to the next level? Or simple dread at the thought of informing the team how stupendously my plan backfired?

CHAPTER TWENTY-FOUR

"I'm speechless," Jeff said – a rare occurrence for him – after I'd informed the team what had happened at Helen's home. We sat in heavy rattan chairs around a circular stone table on the back patio of the rental. It was a bit nippy for the men, but I was dying in the house. The fifty-degree dusk temperature kept me from feeling like I was frying from the inside out. Barely. Thank goodness it was December.

"She really said she has no problem if all cheaters die?" Mandie asked. Her head bobbed on the screen of my cellphone, propped against the pole mounted in the middle of the table for the umbrella. Given the lack of sun, it remained furled.

"She did," I confirmed, before taking a long pull of my ice water. If nothing else, the overheating was resulting in some serious extra hydration. My skin would be baby soft if I didn't die.

"That isn't what I would have predicted," Dan said with a mirthless laugh. "I mean, I didn't think it would work, but—"

"Me neither," Mandie and Jeff added in unison.

"Thanks, guys," I said dryly.

"Sorry, Sarah," Jeff said. "Just trying to commiserate with how horribly it went." At my look, he hurried to clarify. "It's one thing to think it won't work. It's another…" He shrugged.

"I know, I know," I said, before smacking myself in the forehead. "How could I have missed it?"

"What? Missed what?" The questions from the team overlapped.

"During my interview with Natalie in the hospital, there was a brief moment where a hostile energy rose up. I remember fighting a desire to yell. As quick as it was there, it vanished. Then she distracted me and I forgot about it. Until now."

"What do you think it means?" Jeff asked.

"Based on how the conversation between Helen and Natalie went? I'd guess that in the hospital Natalie was still struggling between what she considered the socially acceptable response and wanting to kill her husband."

"We know which part won," Dan said, raising his glass of water with a shrug.

"Yeah, we do," I agreed. "And she must possess some incredible emotional self-control to have buried it so thoroughly that my clairempathy barely registered it. Until the explosion of emotion at Helen's house, of course." My shoulders slumped. If I'd remembered that feeling from Natalie at the hospital, I never would have suggested that she talk to Helen. Jeff touched my shoulder.

"Don't beat yourself up over this. We all agreed to the plan. Sometimes it doesn't go the way we want."

"Thanks, boss."

His eyebrows rose at the word boss, and before I had a moment to consider why, given that I called him that all the time, Dan jumped in with a question.

"Should we call the police?" Jeff and I stared at him, and Mandie tried to angle herself his way. He flushed under the scrutiny. "We have before."

I sighed. "No need to be defensive. We understand where you're coming from."

"What would you tell the police?" Jeff asked. Dan answered in earnest, but I understood Jeff's intent better.

"People have died, and Helen confessed."

"What did Helen confess to?" Jeff asked.

Dan's head swiveled between me and our boss. "Sarah said that she told Natalie she wouldn't stop."

"Not quite. She said if she was responsible, she wouldn't stop. She also said she didn't know if she was responsible," I reminded him.

"Oh, that's true." Dan tapped his foot on a paver. "It just seems…" He trailed off.

"We understand the desire for justice," Jeff said. "But, what would you tell the police? They look for means, motive, and opportunity." Jeff ticked the three off on his fingers. "You'd be stumped at means."

Dan twisted his lips. "I see what you mean."

"It's a good question," Jeff reassured our junior team member. "And you're right that we have before. But we need to consider the effectiveness of such a move."

I bit my lower lip. "Here's the thing, though. Separate from what the police would or could do, there was something, especially toward the end. I don't believe Helen is as heartless as she's letting on."

Dan quirked an eyebrow.

"Seriously. When my feelings – meaning Helen's feelings," I corrected, "of anger and self-righteousness swept through me, I felt other emotions, buried way down deep. Way down."

"Could you identify them?" Mandie asked.

"At first, maybe ambivalence," I said, trying to talk through my thoughts and memories of the experience. "Then, a sense of disquiet."

"That does suggest some level of doubt. Part of her is questioning her path," Jeff mused.

"Exactly." I pointed to Jeff with one hand and placed the forefinger of my other hand on my nose.

"What does that mean for our next approach?" Dan asked. We lapsed into silence at the question.

And then it clicked. "Remorse," I said.

The other three stared at me in confusion.

"Remorse," I repeated. "That was the buried emotion I felt. She may have buried it deep, but once Helen understood she was connected to people dying, even her cheating husband, I suspect, some part of her felt remorse. Likely still feels remorse," I concluded.

"That sounds like a good thing," Mandie said. "How does this help us?"

"My approach was right—" I ignored my teammates' groans. "—but the person was wrong."

"Who would have been better?" Jeff asked. "Isn't Paula Helms the only one left?"

I nodded enthusiastically.

"Not to rain on your parade," Dan said, "but how would it be different with her?"

"Not just her," I answered. "Paula and Cameron." I smacked the table with my right hand and then clutched it close to my body because it hurt. Reining in my enthusiasm would be a good thing.

"He's hospitalized," Jeff reminded me.

"Details," I said with a dismissive wave.

"That's not a detail," he countered.

"I have an idea for that," I assured him. "The first step is convincing Paula."

"Will she go for it?" Dan asked.

"Let's find out. I'm putting you on hold, Mandie."

"Wait," Mandie cried out.

"What?"

"Can you lower your protection to check that she's not, ahem, bamboozling you?"

"Bamboozling?" I asked with an eye roll.

"Forewarned is forearmed?" She offered with a shrug.

"I can't, remember?"

Now Mandie rolled her eyes. "You need physical proximity. Right."

"But, someone else can," I enthused. "Hold on." I typed in a quick text and waited for a response, the eyes of the others trained on me.

"Catherine doesn't need physical proximity," I explained, and a collective *aha* sounded, timed with the notification of an incoming response. "Now I need to pause you, Mandie," I said, after reading it.

I paused the video chat and called Catherine. "Thank you so much for helping us out. On your honeymoon," I added in chagrin.

Her laughter flowed over the line. "I wouldn't have volunteered my help if I didn't mean it," she reassured me.

"You know what we need?" I confirmed.

"Is Paula telling the truth about wanting to help? Got it."

I paused the call and found Paula's number in my phone. A few rings later, she answered.

"Good evening, Paula. This is Sarah Danger. You're on speakerphone with the team." Of course, I left out the fact that a human lie detector was on the call.

"Hi everyone. Do you have any news?" The hopeful tone in her voice strengthened my resolve. This would work.

"I might," I began. "We have a plan to try to undo what has happened to Cameron—"

"Anything," she blurted out.

"Did you mean what you said about wanting to save your marriage?" I asked, though her interruption of my sentence was a strong indicator.

"Yes." We heard a choked sob.

A text appeared on my screen. A thumbs-up emoji from Catherine, which I relayed to the team.

"He's not doing well," Paula continued. "The doctor doesn't know how much longer he has. A day or two at most."

That discouraged me, though I wasn't surprised. I tried for a hopeful tone. "Are you up for doing something that might sound a little unusual?"

"Yes?" Uncertainty had crept into her voice.

"Tonight?"

"The sooner the better," she said in a surer tone.

Another text appeared. Another thumbs-up emoji. I mimicked it to the team.

"Meet us at the hospital in—" I checked my watch. "—twenty minutes. In Cameron's room."

"I'm in the cafeteria, so that won't be a problem."

We disconnected, but I stayed on with Catherine. "Thank you so much for your help."

"That's all you need?"

"She believed what she was saying?"

"Without question."

"That's what we needed. Enjoy the rest of your honeymoon."

I beamed at Jeff and Dan before returning to the paused video chat to catch Mandie up.

"You're going to convince Cameron's doctor to release him, despite being at death's door, and then Paula, Cameron, and the team are going to ambush Helen to convince her that not all cheated-on women want their partners dead, and in fact, some couples want to save their marriages?" Mandie summarized in one very long question.

"I wouldn't use the word ambush," I clarified, ignoring the flabbergasted looks on Jeff's and Dan's faces. "But, yeah, that's the plan. Wish us luck."

"Good luck," Mandie said, shaking her head at me. "You're going to need it."

CHAPTER TWENTY-FIVE

Cameron looked terrible. A permanent line of sweat trailed down both sides of his face. His cracked lips were parted and we could hear wheezy breathing. His skin was bright red, presumably from the feverish temperature; I didn't even want to ask what he was up to now. And the room stank. Dan and I hovered in the doorway, while Paula rushed to her husband's side. His eyes fluttered when she took his hand.

"Hey honey," she whispered.

"What are you doing here?" He croaked out this barely audible question.

"Sarah and the team have an idea."

Well, the team was only me and Dan tonight. Jeff had decided that it really might seem like an ambush if the three of us, plus Cameron and Paula, descended on Helen. We'd even debated about Dan coming. But given my state of worsening physical health, we chose to have at least one additional member of the team present for backup.

Cameron craned his head to try to see around Paula. Dan and I took this as a cue to come closer.

"How are you feeling?" Dan asked.

A dry laugh escaped Cameron's cracked lips. "Like I'm burning up from the inside out. Doctor says my organs are shutting down."

A tear slipped from Paula's eye and she brushed at it. "We have a plan."

"Tell me about it," he said, his gaze jumping between the three of us.

Fatigue stole over me and I wanted nothing more than to sleep. Everything hurt, and it was a chore to keep my eyes open.

Argh, that was Cameron, not me. I focused on the extreme emotions and physical sensations, encasing them in the familiar bubble and releasing them with my next breath.

"Are you okay?" Dan asked, his hand gripping my upper arm.

"Give me a sec," I whispered. A few more deep breaths and I thought I'd isolated what were Cameron's experiences and what were mine. "Okay. Here's the plan." I outlined what I wanted to do, and Cameron grimaced.

"Is that how you really feel?" This question directed at his wife.

"Yes, honey, it is."

"Even though I…" His blazing eyes tracked hers. "Even though I cheated on you."

A wave of conflicting emotions washed over me, and I stepped away to sit in a chair against the back wall. Dan shot me a look of concern before joining me and giving the couple space.

"Yes," Paula answered. "We both have a lot of work to do. If you want to fix our marriage—"

"I do."

"—the first step is to get you well."

"And then?" The naked fear cracked his voice.

"You'll need to end the affair."

"Of course," he agreed.

"And we'll start in therapy."

"Therapy? I've never been in therapy before."

"It'll help us both figure out how we got to this place, and how we can get out of it." She ran a hand through her brown hair and sighed. "One step at a time. What do you think of the plan?"

At her question, Dan and I stepped back to the side of the bed to await Cameron's answer. He thought for a moment.

"Crazy, but I'm game. How are we getting me out of here?"

A stern voice boomed from behind us. "Out of here? What are you talking about?" Paula, Dan, and I turned as one to find Dr. Michael Wilhelm's tall frame in the doorway. His dark eyes narrowed and his bright smile dimmed. "What are you talking about?" he repeated.

"Good to see you, Doctor Wilhelm," I tried for pseudo-jocularity. He frowned. "We need Cameron released."

"Out of the question."

"He'll sign a medical release," I said, familiar with the medical establishment's ever-present concern of being sued.

"Irrelevant."

"How is it irrelevant?" That was a new one. If a patient wanted to be released against medical advice, as long as they weren't a danger to themselves or others— oh, I thought I understood.

"This may be a public health crisis," he said, confirming what I'd realized. His tone softened. "I'm not sure what's going on, but until we understand how this illness is spread, I can't authorize his release. I'm sorry."

"There haven't been any new cases," I argued, ignoring the fact that I was a new case. "And we know it isn't airborne, or there'd be a lot more cases already."

"It's not up to me. It's the public health department."

My mouth fell open. "It's officially a public health crisis?"

"A local one, yes."

We didn't have time to argue with the doctor, so it was time to get rid of him. "Okay, we understand, and we thank you for the information. We won't push for him to be released." I ignored the gasps around me.

"Thank you. Again, I'm sorry. I appreciate your understanding." The doctor proceeded to review

Cameron's chart and check all the equipment attached to him. Beeping increased and slowed. Eyes bored into me, and I ignored them too. The overlapping questions the moment Dr. Wilhelm left the room gave me whiplash.

"What are you doing?"

"What do you mean, you won't push for Cameron to be released?"

"Are we abandoning the plan?"

I held up a hand to stop the barrage. "Of course, we aren't abandoning the plan. The doctor doesn't need to release Cameron. We only needed the doctor to finish his rounds, so he'd go home."

"We're organizing a jailbreak!" Dan exclaimed.

My head bobbed in excitement. "Yes, we are." I crooked a finger at him. "You come with me." I pointed at Paula. "You get him some clothes, unplug the machines." I took a step toward the door and whipped around. "Do NOT simply detach anything from Cameron," I warned, "or you're liable to activate a screeching alarm in the nurse's station." She nodded in understanding.

Dan and I headed into the hallway. "What are we looking for?"

"That," I answered, pointing at a wheelchair far down the long hallway, pushed against the wall. It was equidistant from the rooms on both sides, leaving me to speculate that it wasn't needed by either occupant. I hoped I was right. I'd hate to inconvenience a poor, sick person who needed the chair. We scurried to the wheelchair, peeking in each open door we passed. Everyone seemed to be eating or asleep. I checked my watch and saw it was already after seven. We had to get moving. Helen might not appreciate the interruption, but if we arrived around dinnertime, it was more likely she'd be home.

Dan grabbed the handles of the wheelchair and we hurried down the hallway back to Cameron's room. The silence struck me first. Nothing beeping, no signs of life on any of the unplugged machines. That was good, no wailing alarms. Paula stood next to her husband, who sagged against her. She'd helped him into a short-sleeved shirt, shorts, and sneakers. If not for his death-warmed-over appearance, you'd never guess he was an escaping patient.

Dan and Paula assisted Cameron into the wheelchair and then she moved behind it, intending to push her husband. Dan opened his mouth, and I laid a hand on his forearm. "It's okay."

I poked my head into the hallway. "The way to the elevator is clear. Act like everything we're doing is normal," I instructed them. "Try not to look guilty." I snorted as I took in their guilt-ridden faces. "Let's move."

Dan and I led the way, with Paula pushing Cameron in the wheelchair behind us. We stood before the elevator doors, watching the numbers above increase. We were going to get caught. I knew it. This would be for nothing. My head pounded with the fear of failing. I sucked in a breath. My sickness was making my protection barrier tenuous.

"Everyone calm down. It's going to be fine." The emotions began to recede, and I was merely overheated and slightly nauseous when we entered the elevator. The decreased intensity of the emotions buoyed me. We exited the elevator on the ground floor and moved with purpose toward the sliding glass doors to freedom.

"Excuse me?"

"Keep going," I whispered to Dan. He dropped back to stand beside Paula and they kept moving as a block toward the exit.

I, on the other hand, pivoted to address the owner of the voice, a nurse wearing blue scrubs and a nametag that said Susie. "Can I help you?"

"Has that man been checked out?" The nurse pointed at the retreating trio. She was merely questioning, at least, not accusatory. I could work with that.

"Would we be taking him home if he wasn't?" I asked, sidestepping the question, and not technically lying.

"I didn't see any paper or nurse," she apologized.

"No problem. It's good to check. Better safe than sorry," I assured her with a wide grin.

She smiled back. "Hope he's doing okay."

"He will be," I said, hoping I was right. "Thank you so much for your concern. Mahalo."

"Mahalo," she replied and returned to the desk from which she'd materialized.

I scooted through the sliding glass doors, thrilled to see Dan with the empty wheelchair. "He's in the SUV?"

"Ready to go." Dan disappeared through the sliding glass doors. I rushed to the SUV two rows away. I pulled open the driver's side door, nodded to Cameron and Paula in the backseat, and put the vehicle in reverse. Dan met the SUV one row over, hopped into the front passenger seat.

"Is everybody ready?" I asked. My heart rate, anxiety, and stomach all jumped in response. I focused on the kernel of hope mixed in with the worry… at least someone had a higher level of confidence. I swallowed hard past a lump in my burning throat. This would work.

It had to.

CHAPTER TWENTY-SIX

The SUV slowed to a stop in Helen Richards' driveway. We stared at her sky-blue two-story home, lit up by security lights like a beacon in the night. Before exiting the vehicle, I considered the combined impact of acutely-ill Cameron and malice-filled Helen on my clairempathy. Especially in my physically-weakened state. I wanted to hone in on the layer of Helen's emotions that hinted she was open to what we'd be suggesting. But taking a chance on the emotional and physical responses of the group incapacitating me was too high. It would be best to shore up my psychic defenses.

"I need a minute," I said to the group. "If you want to help Cameron up the stairs, though, that would be good," I suggested to Paula and Dan. I remained seated while the doors opened, words of encouragement were murmured, and doors closed.

Instead of the bubble I used to release others' emotions, this time I visualized the familiar wall. My stone wall, something that would not be out of place surrounding a medieval castle, except rising into the sky. Nothing would get over or around it. Eyes closed, I inhaled and exhaled several slow, measured breaths. My eyes opened to see that my companions had reached the top of the stairs and waited under the gazebo portion of the porch. I hurried to join them and knocked on the door.

None of us likely missed the flash of surprise and then irritation at finding us on her doorstep. "Apologies for the late intrusion," I offered before she could close the door in our faces.

An imperceptible sigh. "What can I do for you this time?" To be honest, Helen didn't appear well. Her blond hair hung limply around her face, which was sallow with what appeared to be angry acne forming. Her eyes were the only things showing life, and they almost glowed – internal energy, anger, or something supernatural?

"This is my teammate, Dan," I said, gesturing at the young man, who lifted a hand in greeting. "And these two are Cameron and Paula Helms."

I watched Helen's eyes take in the three, stopping the longest on Cameron, who of course, looked like he was dying.

"As you can see, Cameron isn't doing well. In fact, Cameron is dying." I deliberately repeated his name when explaining. It was a tactic I'd heard law enforcement used when negotiating with a hostage taker to humanize the victim. Weird to think of Helen in those terms, yet it seemed accurate. Her anger was holding us hostage.

Helen's eyes softened for a moment and she turned back toward the house. "You might as well come in."

We hustled to stay with her before she could change her mind. Dan closed the door behind us, and our little caravan returned to the living room. Helen perched again on her white wicker chair. Cameron, Paula, and I sat on the couch. Dan remained standing, off to the side, more observer than participant.

"You don't look so good, either," Helen noted.

"Thanks," I replied dryly. "I've been better. It seems you weren't wrong about my risking getting ill. I'm probably on the same trajectory as Cameron. Who. Is. Dying," I emphasized. She flinched as though struck and, despite my wall of protection, I flinched in unison. Her emotions had to be amplified by something. A goddess's power, perhaps?

"I've already told you. People deserve whatever they get. There are consequences for behavior." The words were as assured, but the uncertainty beneath them surfaced and my breath caught in my throat. It was like my wall didn't even exist for Helen. This could be tricky.

I nodded at her statement. "True. I thought it might be... helpful for you to hear from someone affected by what's happening."

She sneered, but I saw through her veneer at this point. "Didn't you learn from your last failed attempt at this?"

"This one is a little different." I placed a hand on Paula's which sat on Cameron's. "Are you ready?" They nodded.

"Thank you for agreeing to see us," Paula began, and Cameron held up a hand for her to stop. "Yes, honey?"

"May I go first?" he rasped out. When Paula nodded, he continued. "I made a mistake. A horrible, horrible mistake." He squeezed his wife's hand though didn't break eye contact with Helen. "You aren't wrong that there are consequences to actions. The consequences to my actions were to hurt the woman I love, and another woman I care about."

Helen's anger flared, and I wondered about the wisdom of mentioning the lover so casually. Oh well, too late.

"I felt adrift in my marriage and instead of speaking with my wife, like the partner I vowed to be, I found what seemed to be an easier route. That was wrong. I can't overstate that. I love my wife." He wiped sweat from his forehead and faced Paula. "I love you. And I hope to spend the rest of my life making this up to you, showing you how much I love you."

Paula brushed tears from her cheek. "I love you too." She turned to Helen, whose anger was rapidly cooling. "Don't misunderstand. I'm not ready to forgive him yet. But I'd like the opportunity to try."

Paula aimed a crooked smile at Cameron. "Whether or not we make it through this as a couple, Cameron doesn't deserve to die."

"You said you may not forgive him?" Helen questioned in a low voice. Her hands clutched at the arms of the chair.

"Yes. I may not. But it's my choice. Not yours." She dropped her volume to match Helen's. "What you're doing isn't what I want. You aren't helping me. Please stop whatever it is that's causing this. Please don't kill my husband." Tears flowed in streams down Paula's cheeks now, her bloodshot eyes beseeching Helen.

"I don't know if I can," Helen whispered.

CHAPTER TWENTY-SEVEN

Pain seared my insides. Guilt flooded through me. I had to make amends. I had to fix this. People were dying – no, had already died! – because of me. Tears filled my eyes and tracked down my cheeks in concert with Helen's.

Voices asked me if I was okay, but I was drowning in Helen's intense emotional and physical reaction to Paula's plea. My protective barrier disintegrated like it had never existed.

I leaned over my lap, head between my knees, gulping in air. Knowing I wasn't going to be able to hold back, I jumped to my feet and stumbled to Helen's kitchen. I thought I heard voices calling out, but I was desperate to get to the sink. My hands gripped the countertop and my head dipped, bumping the bronze faucet spout. Burning acid rose up and spewed into the sink.

"Sarah?"

I waved my hand behind me at Dan to go away, but didn't hear anything in response while I heaved more burning liquid, mostly bile and water. When did I last eat? A few final ragged breaths and then my spasming stomach ceased. After running water and slurping some through a cupped hand, I focused on rebuilding my wall. My ragged breaths became more even. My heart rate slowed. The need to vomit further receded as the wall rose higher in my mind.

When I stood from the sink, Dan still remained in the doorway. His eyes reflected understanding. He followed me to the living room, where the others stared in shock at me. Dan and I retook our seats.

"Apologies. I guess I'm not feeling well, either," I said, not wanting to delve into the nature of clairempathy at this moment. Not when we'd had a breakthrough with Helen. I reached across the coffee table to take Helen's hands, which she accepted. Perhaps my vomiting into her sink had sparked some additional sympathy. "I know how horrible you feel. I understand how lost you are."

"What do I need to do? How can I fix this?" Her grip on my hands tightened with the questions before she released mine and hugged her middle.

I considered her questions, and the team's earlier speculation. Here was a moment of truth. If Helen was the sole cause, and we could move her away from revenge, then Cameron and I should improve. "Our team researched some possibilities, and we have an idea of steps to try."

"Anything." She removed a tissue from the box on the table and blew her nose, before tucking the used tissue in a pocket of her Capri pants.

"The first step is to perform, or offer, a prayer for forgiveness."

"Forgiveness?"

"Of your husband, Alan. And of yourself."

"Oh." She looked at her hands, now fidgeting in her lap.

"Helen, look at me." She complied. "Do you want the harm to stop?"

"Yes," she answered without hesitation.

"We don't know exactly how this is happening," I admitted. "But since your anger appears connected to—" I quickly debated reminding her Pele may be connected and decided not to. "—a supernatural illness, this is a possible first step."

She took a shaky breath. "Okay, I'm ready."

"This is a Hawaiian ritual known as ho'oponopono. It consists of a series of four powerful statements to bring the speaker toward forgiveness and healing. It's a way to make things right." I waved my hand, trying to find the words from my earlier research. "Sort of like a mantra or meditation."

"I enjoy meditation," Helen said with a nod.

"The idea behind the four sentences is to become right within yourself and right within the world." I hesitated to add, *and hopefully calm down Pele*. "Repeat after me. *I am sorry.*"

HEATHER SILVIO

"I am sorry," she said, her voice almost inaudible.

"What are you sorry for?"

Tears overflowed her blue eyes again. "I'm sorry I allowed my anger at my husband to hurt others."

"Now repeat, *Please forgive me.*"

"Please forgive me," she repeated, her voice stronger.

"Forgive you for what?" I prompted.

"Forgive me for refusing your offer to fix this once I realized I was causing harm." She nodded at me.

The next question wasn't part of the technique, yet it felt right to include. "Are you able to forgive Alan?"

A small sad laugh bubbled up. "I think eventually. He made mistakes. Like you did," she said to Cameron. "I don't know if we could have recovered from it. We'd been unhappy in our marriage for a long time. And I felt like an idiot. But he didn't deserve to die; I didn't know then that I was causing harm—" She stopped herself. "It's not about excuses. Although I didn't know then, I certainly allowed my anger to overwhelm me and celebrated his death. That's not okay. And something I'll have to live with."

Compassion welled within me for Helen's turmoil. "Next statement: *Thank you.* Not to or for anything specific, but for you, Alan, us. Learning about what happened and the opportunity to undo it," I added.

"Thank you." She closed her eyes, and we watched her lips move as she murmured to herself her expression of thanks. Her eyes reopened, and I swore they seemed more at peace.

"And, finally, *I love you.*"

She frowned. "Who is that directed to? Alan?"

I shook my head. "As before, it's to everything and everyone. Yourself, Alan, the universe. Find the love and direct it outward."

"I love you," she said, slowly and distinctly. "I love you."

"How do you feel?" I asked.

"Better. Lighter, somehow."

I opened myself up to her, removing a few of the stones from my towering wall. I too was lighter, still a bit of guilt and disappointment in myself, but better now that I could move forward. Helen and I exchanged smiles. I replaced the stones, and with the removal of her clarity and lightness, I slumped against Paula.

"Sarah!" Dan cried out.

Voices receded, though hands touched me, trying to determine if I was okay. As if at a distance, I also heard someone – probably Paula – call out to Cameron.

This wasn't good. My insides were boiling and my stomach rocked with nausea. I worried I would pass out, so I removed a few stones from my wall again. Introducing Helen's positivity overcame my illness and the worry of the others around me. I recovered enough to sit up.

"What's happening?" Helen asked.

"Shouldn't Cameron be getting better?" Paula's question overlapped.

I nodded, creating a wave of dizziness. "Let's try something more."

"Of course," Helen agreed.

I thought about the research we'd seen regarding forgiveness. "Forgiveness includes three types of transgressions." I wracked my brain for the names. "Hala is an error of omission. Hewa is an error of excess. And 'ino is intentional harm."

The others were looking at me with such expectation; I needed to make this make sense. "Your anger and the results sort of followed this path, right?"

"Yes, I think I get it," Helen said. "My anger at Alan became excessive, leading to consequences I didn't know about, a type of omission. But," she swallowed audibly, "when I did, I didn't care and I wished for intentional harm." Sadness rose in her, and because my walls were a bit lowered, in me.

"But you've started the process of forgiving Alan and yourself," I reminded her. "Try forgiving each of these transgressions. The whole path you took." I felt better, and I didn't know if that was her or me. "Does that even make sense?"

"I believe so." She collected her thoughts. "I will work on forgiving Alan for his transgressions, and I forgive myself for mine. I don't want revenge. I don't want to punish anyone." She looked around, as though seeking another presence. "I don't want anyone else to be hurt."

I glanced at Cameron. He didn't seem any different. Paula's frenetic anxiety was bouncing off my wall of protection, which I'd raised at the influence of Helen's sadness. This was all exhausting, to be honest. I just wanted to go to bed.

"Why isn't it working?" Paula begged me for an answer.

I floundered for a moment. And then decided now was the time to tell Helen our alternate theory. "Do you remember what I said during happy hour? This may sound crazy," I said to her, "but our second theory was that you have a connection to Pele."

"I have a what?" Helen asked, her voice rising on the last word. "I don't really remember our conversation."

"A connection to Pele," I repeated.

Her hands covered her mouth for a moment and then her arms sprung wide. "I don't know what to do with that."

"We need to soothe Pele." Despite my attempt at a matter-of-fact tone, Helen's eyebrows rose skyward. "Help her realize her assistance is no longer required," I continued. "And I have a bit of a harebrained scheme, if you're up for it."

"Another one?" Dan asked with a smirk.

CHAPTER TWENTY-EIGHT

It had been nine days since Cameron Helms developed symptoms and two days since I did. Now I sat in the front passenger seat of the SUV, hoping my crazy plan would work. Based on Cameron's state when we left Helen's house last night, I doubted he'd make it much longer, a hunch Paula confirmed when we checked in this morning. He was bedridden, struggling to breathe. She guessed his lungs were failing from his relentless high internal temperature. He'd said no when she asked him if he wanted to go back to the hospital. They both were ignoring frantic calls from the hospital and instead praying for our success.

I, thankfully, felt better; separating from the much sicker Cameron allowed me to ditch at least his physical symptoms, which had overpowered me last night. Between

Helen's emotions and Cameron's illness, I was lucky I hadn't stayed passed out.

Helen sat in the back seat. I could see her in the passenger-side mirror; she remained quiet and stared out the window while we drove to the park. We'd picked her up at dawn. She was at peace, prepared for whatever came next if her emotional and physical energy were accurate. By tapping into her energy and Dan's very positive sense of wellbeing, I shored up my own. My insides were boiling, but at least the healthy energy diluted it some. My symptoms seemed disproportionally worse given the short timeframe, leaving me to wonder if my clairempathy was amplifying the effects somehow.

Our plan was to repeat the hike that Dan and I had completed earlier. We entered the park, drove past the Kīlauea Visitor Center, and continued on Crater Rim Drive to the Steam Vents parking lot. The orange cones still blocked the road beyond the lot entrance. Plenty of spots remained open this early on a cloudy day. Dan parked in one and we exited the vehicle. I pulled my hat lower over my ears out of habit and then immediately yanked it back off. Staying warm would not be an issue.

"Are you ready?" I asked my companions. They understood I didn't just mean for the hike.

A spike of anxiety crested and receded. They both nodded. We kept close to Crater Rim Drive until reaching the sign for the Kīlauea Military Camp. Like before, we headed inward toward the caldera to pick up the Crater Rim Trail.

Helen, Dan, and I picked our way around cracks and sinkholes. We hiked with purpose, but I made sure to touch the waist-high scrub brush and smaller trees we passed. It seemed important to stay in contact with nature before attempting what we planned. I stumbled, and Dan's hand on my arm kept me from falling.

"Are you okay?"

Déjà vu rocked me, and I hesitated before answering. "Just lost my footing." Except it was more than that. The fatigue that had been held at bay by the two's energy had surged. My bones felt heavy. The need to sleep was nearly all-consuming. I felt disoriented and confused, unsure of my actions. I abruptly halted and they stopped beside me.

"What is it?" Helen whispered.

I glanced around and shook my head. "I sense another. Different from before." Dan and Helen waited while I separated what I felt from my own emotions. "No hostility. Something has definitely changed."

"The impact of the ho'oponopono?" Helen asked.

"Probably," I answered, coughing. The smell of ash had risen, though the tickling in my throat seemed more than a physical reaction. I didn't recognize our location, but I knew we were close. "This way," I said with utter confidence. Bigger fissures came into view and we proceeded with caution. Charred plants became more abundant. Odd. Would there be charring without obvious lava? Of course, this was not an entirely natural event.

A faint glow appeared in the distance. "We're almost there," Dan shouted, and déjà vu rocked me again.

There was no point in continuing. I was lost and so confused. What was I supposed to be doing? I'd been so angry, but now frustration flowed. "Wait," I said, and then turned in a circle. My arms extended like I was feeling my way in the dark. Which in a sense I was. This wasn't right.

"I'm not sure what's going on," Helen murmured. "But I don't think this is you."

Dan reached out and clasped my hands. "Doc. Sarah. Whatever you're experiencing, these aren't your perceptions or emotions."

"Not yet," I mumbled before passing out.

"Sarah. Can you hear me? Sarah?"

Dan's voice found me in the internal darkness of my mind and brought me back to awareness. I sat on the rough ground, idly thankful for the tough material of my hiking pants, leaning against Dan. I pitched forward and dry heaved.

"Sarah!" Helen's cry drew my attention.

I held a hand up to keep both of them away. When I steadied enough, I pushed myself off the ground and lurched to my feet. Graceful, I'm sure. "It's okay," I assured them. "For the moment anyway." This repeated crumbling of my defensive barrier was getting old. Maybe I needed a new image. Sheesh. I closed my eyes, focusing on restacking my stone wall, imagining it towering over me. I needed the protection, at least until we made it to some actual lava.

"We have to find an active lava flow to interact with Pele," I explained to the others.

"Interact?" Helen asked.

"What did you think we were going to do?" Dan countered dryly.

Her cheeks tinged pink.

"Just teasing," he rushed to add.

"I wasn't being metaphorical last night when I told you we needed to calm Pele down," I explained to Helen. "I'm a clairempath. That means I experience the emotional and physical reactions of those around me. Something is here."

As I spoke the words with such confidence, part of me wondered if it was true.

Could it be solely Helen, reacting to being present where we believed it all began? I cleared my mind and focused on tapping into the surrounding energy. Like dipping a toe in the pool, as opposed to the belly flop I'd had moments before.

"This way," I said, and we continued. After thirty minutes, everything shot up. My temperature, fatigue, and the power trying to find a path around my defenses.

"We must be close," Dan declared with a groan. "This is how I felt last time."

Helen pointed. "Look! Lava."

The lava glowed as it bubbled and grew. It struck me again how amazing the birth of new earth looked. We stood about twenty feet away. The energy flowing around me threatened my protective barrier. It was now or never.

"I'm going to lower my wall," I told the others. "Be ready to follow my lead." They nodded and stepped back.

I faced the lava and inhaled, hoping I remembered enough from our research to do this adequately and respectfully.

While holding my hands out to the sides, I visualized removing stones from my wall. The energy that had been poking and prodding flooded into me once there was an opening. Anger and hostility remained present, but confusion and frustration overtook them. I kept a careful internal eye on the feelings, trying not to let them overwhelm me again.

"Tutu Pele," I began, using the honorific. "Ka wahine 'ai honus," I continued with her poetic name. "We know you are the woman who devours the land. We understand you answered Helen's call for retribution," I said, then stopped when a wave of anger rocked me backward.

"Balance," I corrected. "A misdeed was done and you responded. You helped," I assured her. "It's time now to restore balance the other way. People are dying. People have died." I held a moment of silence for those who hadn't made it, then nodded at Helen, who picked up my cue.

"Thank you for helping me. I've been cleansed and found my balance. I'm ready to move forward."

Energy rippled over my skin, the sense of uncertainty rising. "Keep going. You're on the right track," I encouraged her.

"Please, Tutu Pele," she continued, repeating my use of the honorific. "I thank you for your assistance and ask that you return to your own balance." She fumbled the last words, possibly unsure what to say, but I thought she got her point across.

I opened myself up wide to the energy within. The raw power engulfed me, driving me to my knees. This time there was no nausea, no headache, nothing negative. Light filled me. Peace filled me. The confusion and frustration blinked out of existence. I sat cross-legged on the earth, placed my hands palms up on my knees, and closed my eyes. Helen had fallen silent. I listened with my soul to the sounds of the goddess and the earth until every bit of the energy faded. My eyes opened and I took in the surrounding scene. While we watched in fascination, the lava stopped bubbling before us. The sun's rays pushed through the clouds. It was like a switch had been flipped. Unreal.

"Is this really happening?" Helen asked in awe.

"I think so," Dan answered her in a low voice.

Scrambling to my feet, I turned to face my companions.

"Oh wow," Helen said.

"What?" I touched myself to confirm I had all my body parts. Was something wrong?

"You're glowing," Dan said, eyes round as saucers.

Huh, that was new. "Helen," I said, choosing not to address this unforeseen consequence. "For whatever reason, you are tied into supernatural energy. Do you know what that means?"

"Not at all," she responded with a shaky laugh.

"There are many things outside our ability to explain them. This is probably always going to be one of them." I tried not to sound like I was giving a lecture. "My best guess is that the combination of Alan's cheating and your affinity for Hawaiian culture somehow manifested previously latent paranormal or supernatural abilities."

"Oh my." She chewed on her lower lip. "What do I do?"

"We have friends in the paranormal community. If you're open to it, we can connect you to some of them and they can help you hone in on your own skills and abilities."

She nodded like a bobble-head. "Yes, please."

"Of course."

"So I can develop my powers for good?"

Relief filled me as her hope and transition – telling a joke! – buoyed me up. "Yes." I started back the way we came. "One thing I'm not certain of, that I still feel the need to mention, is what happened with Natalie."

"What do you mean?"

"I don't understand how, any more than I understand much of this," I said. "It may be that you enhanced her desire to punish her husband when we came to meet you."

Helen's hand on my upper arm stopped my forward motion. Her eyes had widened. "Is that why she did her about-face?"

I lifted a single shoulder in a small shrug. "That's my best guess. Watch for it happening in the future." I chuckled. "It's a lot, to watch for others, along with your own, but you'll get used to it. Mostly."

"But what is it?"

"You may have the ability now to focus and direct emotions that mirror yours. Somehow, the intense negativity associated with Alan cheating on you the second time brought all that latent skill right on up to the surface."

"So, I'll really need to work on managing my own emotions," she said. "No pressure there."

I embraced her. "You can do this."

"Thanks," she murmured into my hair.

We separated and began walking again. "Let's get to the hospital and see how everyone is doing. I know I've never felt this good in my life." How could I put these feelings into words? Happiness flooded through me. My skin felt alive. The very air never smelled so invigorating. I honestly felt in touch with the lifeforce of the world. "I feel invincible," I summarized instead.

"Literally glowing would do that for you, I imagine," Dan joked.

CHAPTER TWENTY-NINE

Texts flew back and forth between the team while Dan drove our group to our respective houses. Although I felt better, I initially wasn't sure if I was somehow basking in leftover goddess glow. We'd confirmed quite a few things, however, by the time we'd reached Helen's adorable sky-blue two-story home.

Paula Helms reported that Cameron's temperature had fallen several degrees, and he appeared on the road to an almost full recovery; there had been scarring on his lungs that would plague him, especially as he aged. But he was thankful to be alive. Patricia Elliott was recovering, though devastated when Cameron broke up with her to start the hard work of repairing his marriage.

Kevin Christian was also recovering and, although Natalie recanted her previous wish for him to die, he planned to file for divorce from her as soon as he was able. He hoped it would be amicable, for the sake of the children, and planned to ask for joint custody. When he expressed some concern about her vindictive nature, I cautioned him to consider what had preceded it.

And, finally, Dr. Michael Wilhelm acknowledged there were no other patients with matching symptoms. No more had appeared once the hiking access had been closed – I supposed not too many people like us ignored the closure. Or who did, but weren't cheating on a partner, I further supposed. Either way, he and the governmental agencies who'd been brought in declared the public health emergency concluded, without ever finding a cause.

Our plea to Pele had worked.

The SUV stopped in Helen's driveway. Dan stayed inside while I walked her to the stairs. She wrapped her arms around me, the scent of vanilla and sweat enveloping me, before stepping away and digging her toe in the gravel.

"Thank you so much. For not giving up and for helping me find my way back."

"You're welcome." I squeezed her hand. "Everybody deserves a second chance."

Her eyes clouded. "I'll spend the rest of my life making up for the lives I cost."

"I know you will."

She stared at me, biting her lower lip.

"Was there something else?"

"Should I turn myself in?" Her gaze shifted over my shoulder.

Ah. I should have expected this. We regained eye contact when I clasped her hands. "What would that look like?" I asked.

"What do you mean?"

"Can you imagine how that conversation would go?" Much as Jeff and I had with Dan, she needed to understand why there couldn't be a legal result in this situation.

Her brow furrowed. "I would ... could ... yeah," she said when the realization hit home. "I see what you mean."

"The best outcome is what you've pledged to do – live your life and make up for what happened. You may have stumbled, but when it mattered, you stepped up," I reminded her.

"Thank you, Sarah," she repeated. We hugged again, briefer this time. She gave a half-wave to Dan before walking up the stairs. When she reached the gazebo, I turned around and returned to the car.

Dan stayed quiet during the drive to our rental house. I lowered my protective barrier and immediately sensed a questioning energy. After raising the wall back up, I considered asking him if there was something on his mind. Nah. I snuggled in the seat, watching the small town of Mountain Eden go by. He'd ask me when he was ready.

Jeff came around the side of the house while we were parking. "I set up for some afternoon cocktails to celebrate. It's out back."

I debated showering first, and decided celebrating sounded better. Dan and I followed him to the patio. The gray pavers practically sparkled in the bright sun. We took seats at the circular stone table, on which sat a pitcher. "Margaritas?" Dan asked.

"Sure, why not?"

"Tropical enough." I laughed.

Jeff filled our glasses.

"How are you feeling?" I asked, taking in his heartier color and regular breathing.

"Pretty good. I'll still follow up with my doctor when we get home," he assured us.

"I never doubted that," Dan replied. "Chrissie would make certain you did."

We clinked our drinks. "To loved ones who care," Jeff toasted.

"To the best team a gal could work with," I added.

"To a free trip to Hawaii," Dan joked. We laughed, of course. Then he grew serious. "I do have a question."

"Shoot." I suspected where he was heading.

"I definitely felt incredible power both times we hiked the volcano," he started. He described the scene to Jeff, who listened with rapt attention. "And I have no doubt there was a supernatural element at play…"

"Spit it out, young man," our boss said.

"Do you believe that we communicated with Pele?" He asked in a rush of words. "Not discounting what we went through," he continued. "But could it have been just an incredible manifestation of Helen's own not-so-latent abilities?"

"I wondered the same thing," I admitted. "Is it possible that Helen may have used her idea of Pele to release some of her responsibility for people dying? To project that responsibility onto an *other*?"

"I must never forget you have a counseling degree," Jeff said.

I chuckled. "Sorry. It's natural at this point."

"No need to apologize," he dismissed. "It's fascinating to think about the possibilities."

"Right," Dan concurred. "Helen was a critical piece of the puzzle, either way."

"Yes. On the one hand, Helen's subconscious mind could have used what she knew of Pele to first cause the damage and then distance herself from that damage. Or, on the other hand, her unknown-to-her supernatural abilities could have woken up Pele, who chose to become involved in a spurned woman's desire for revenge."

"Well, Pele is known for her jealousy and retributive nature," Dan added.

"Retributive?" I asked, quirking an eyebrow.

"I'm a grad student, too. You don't get all the fifty-cent vocab words, doc."

"Not yet," I quipped, then took a sip from my margarita, which soothed my parched but perfectly normal-temperature throat. "We'll never know for sure."

We sat in companionable silence, each deep in thought. I was looking forward to returning home in the morning. Clear weather was forecast, and we expected smooth sailing, as the saying went, for our flight.

But I had a lot to think about on our 15-hour return to Tampa.

CHAPTER THIRTY

In our three-seat row on the Hawaiian Airlines flight, Jeff snoozed on one side of me and Dan had the window. Yes, I was in the middle.

"Whatcha working on?" Dan asked, peeking at the screen of my laptop, no doubt trying to read my open document. I checked out the open document on his screen in return.

"Dissertation. You?"

"Blog." He shifted to face me. "Are you going to finish that bad boy and become Doctor Danger?"

I rolled my eyes. "That's the goal. I'm thrilled to be nearing the end."

"Is this case going to be in it?"

"Oh yeah," I answered. "Most of it is theoretical, talking about how supernatural phenomena may explain many of the more outlandish mythological tales across cultures. But this case was definitely not theoretical, so it's a strong closing."

"Makes sense. That's how I feel about the blog. Although I chronicled some of our interesting cases, I'm excited for the supernatural ones."

"Ones?"

"This will be the first of many, I have no doubt."

Jeff snuffled and sat forward. "I agree. And, Sarah, you did great. You'll do well."

I frowned. "I'll do well? That makes it sound like you won't be there too."

He lifted his drink, which was a cappuccino since it was still before noon. "To your next adventure."

"To *our* next adventure," I corrected, lifting my coffee.

Dan's eyes ricocheted between the two of us. I guess he hadn't been apprised of Jeff's thoughts on retirement.

"Sarah, you know I'm planning to retire," he said gently.

"And I'm not interested in getting a private investigator license," I argued.

"You won't have to."

"I won't have to?"

He shook his head and shifted in his seat to face me. "Despite my teasing you about it, I do understand that you neither want the PI business nor are you prepared to take over. You're sort of like a perpetual PI intern," he joked. Dan and I laughed in response.

"Then I really don't understand."

"How did it go, calling yourself a consultant?"

"It went well," I admitted. "But that seems like quite a gray area. To operate as a PI yet not be a PI."

Jeff shook his head. "I disagree. You wouldn't investigate people, per se, like for insurance fraud or marital infidelity, where it would indeed be illegal. If you're clear that you're not operating as a private investigator, but that you can consult on the, ahem, more unusual cases, I see no legal issues."

"Sort of a supernatural consultant," Dan chimed in.

"I'll think about it," I said with finality. With a wink, Jeff let the matter drop and Dan returned to working on his blog, angling in his seat such that I could no longer view his open document.

This was exactly what I'd started considering last night after we solved the case. This was fun. This was fascinating. Jeff was correct that I didn't want to be a licensed PI. There were a lot of steps I'd have needed to have taken already if that had been a true goal.

Once I finished my dissertation and became Doctor Danger, however, I could become an Adjunct Professor which would leave time for a different type of additional employment. A clairempath with a background in investigative techniques, counseling psychology, and comparative mythology seemed almost predestined to also be a supernatural consultant.

What would I call myself?

Doctor Danger – Supernatural Consultant. Nah, sounds like a superhero bureaucrat.

Doctor Danger – Paranormal PI. Nope, can't use the words, even abbreviated.

Doctor Danger – Mythological Mysteries. Hmm, perhaps too confusing.

Although, looking at those discarded options, I wondered if I should remove my name. It read like a supervillain. I could keep it simple. But that seemed boring. Where's the fun in having the name Danger if you weren't going to use it?

Doctor Sarah Danger – Supernatural Specialist. Providing Supernatural Solutions.

Yeah, that might work. I emailed the possible new name and slogan to Dan, and he gave me a distracted thumbs up to acknowledge receipt.

Two minutes later, an email popped up and I shot a surprised look at my teammate. He smirked and said, "Click the link."

I did, and it brought me to an internet landing page, with DRAFT in big letters across the top. Guess that meant it wasn't fully live yet. Below that, the title:

A Doctor Danger Mystery

Welcome to my new blog! If it defies explanation, call Sarah Danger, Supernatural Specialist. Her team explains the unexplainable, providing supernatural solutions.

I grinned at Dan and settled in to read about our adventure, knowing more would come.

AUTHOR'S NOTE

One of the great joys of writing fiction is being able to create whatever world you want. In setting Sarah's first supernatural mystery on the actual Big Island of Hawai'i, I used real places, such as the Hilo airport and medical center, Kona, and Volcanoes National Park. But I wholly made up the town of Mountain Eden and all of its citizens and businesses.

While I researched this book via the internet, of course, I also flew to Hawaii to hike many of the park's trails. Plus, I really did get within fifteen feet of bubbling lava!

Huge thank you, in particular, to the National Park Service and Hawai'i Volcanoes National Park for the information provided (even if they didn't know I was researching a book). Any errors made are mine alone, or were details changed for the story.

Note, finally, that I chose not to italicize any of the Hawaiian words, as in Hawaii, the native language is equal to English.

I hope you enjoyed coming along on the first of Sarah's adventures, and that you, too, can enjoy the wonders of Hawaii in your travels.

THANK YOU!

Thank you so much for supporting my work and reading this novel.

If you liked the book, please consider leaving a review online.

Just a few lines would be great. Reviews are not only the highest compliment you can pay to an author, they also help other readers discover and make more informed choices about purchasing books in a crowded online space. Thank you so much in advance.

If you didn't like the book or have concerns, please email me directly at
heather@heathersilvio.com

ABOUT THE AUTHOR

Heather Silvio loves to tell stories, especially fun, flirty, fantasy romance & mystery. She is also an actress and licensed psychologist with a few nonfiction titles for variety. When she isn't working, she channels her inner flapper as a 1920s jazz and blues singer.

Visit https://www.heathersilvio.com for more information and to sign up for her New Releases and Appearances Newsletter.

Made in the USA
Columbia, SC
30 July 2022

64082525R00119